Rough & Ready
Copyright©2013 Barry Lowe
ISBN 978-1-909934-10-8
Cover art and design by Dawné Dominique

First published by loveyoudivine Alterotica

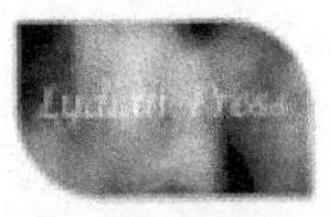

Published by
Lydian Press 2013
Find us on the World Wide Web at
www.lydianpress.com

ROUGH & READY

GAY TOUGH GUY EROTICA

Barry Lowe

Lydian Press

CONTENTS

All the above titles were originally published as individual eBooks by loveyoudivine Alterotica.

† *Climbing up the Wall* was first published in *Hard Hats: Gay Erotic Stories*, edited by Neil Plakcy (Cleis Press, 2008) in a slightly shorter version

INTRODUCTION:

Not everyone wants a love life smothered with vanilla and wrapped in ribbons and valentines – some like it spontaneous, dirty and low-down with the wild ones of the world, with the rebels without a cause. Sweet and sensitive is boring, while those men who take what they want when it's least expected can have a strange addictive lure. Men whose jobs present them with ample opportunity for access to people's homes and beds: those muscular, horny males stripped to the waist with dirt under their fingernails, and thick hard cocks under their jeans.

Alpha males are top of the fantasy fodder food chain. Guys with scars, tattoos and piercings, tough working-class men who aren't afraid to get down and dirty, ex-cons and skinheads who reek of danger and hard, crude sex. These guys are always ready to pop a load; anywhere, anytime, anyhow. In this hot collection of Barry Lowe's hardest erotica, you'll meet a cross section of tough guys, such as the former prison inmate who breaks into a young student's room expecting to find his girlfriend who has long since departed. Or the guy, brutally robbed, who runs into his mugger in a supermarket; the intimidating skinhead who lives in the apartment above a frightened gay couple; the razor gang thug who is forced to fight for his life among the debris of the Depression; the graffiti artist who lives by his wits on the streets and in public toilets but whose secret life is discovered by his brother's violent gang; the plumber who is greeted at the door by a writer dressed in drag because he works under a woman's name; the Wall Street financier who resorts to bondage to wreak his revenge on the co-worker he fancies; the builder who tries subterfuge to seduce his workmate and also the man whose house he is repairing; and, the ex-con who will do anything to turn his sister's boyfriend.

Some of these tough guys are the stuff of nightmares: you wouldn't want to run into them in a dark alley. But between the pages of a book they are the stuff of fantasy - they'll get you good and hard while you read of their adventures.

Barry Lowe
Sydney, Australia

STOCKS AND SHARED

I had him where I wanted him, the arrogant little shit; his head and wrists stuck tight in faux medieval wooden stocks, his body bent forward uncomfortably so that his ass was vulnerable to any passing stray cock. And, boy, did that asshole enjoy stray cock, even though he was the bright, golden future boy of Kensington, Cletus and DeCoteau, investment bankers to the financial gentry.

Recently, he had earned the company the dollar equivalent of the Gross National Income of a middling European Nation, after having been with the firm a scant fifteen months. He was a whiz at the market: the stocks he bought turned to pure gold, and those he sold turned to dross. His future was as bright as his Futures portfolio. So, I guess, he had a lot to be arrogant about.

He was demonically handsome. Envy had it that he had commissioned a well known artist to paint his portrait and the result was stored in his attic. His thick, burnished russet hair reflected his fiery personality, and his piercing green eyes could see through weakness, scams and bullshit like Superman through brick. To make it even more unfair on the rest of us mere mortals who had to sweat for a living, Mitch Badham was athletic, good at social sports, tennis, golf and squash, aided immeasurably by powerful tanned legs with a dusting of light hair like icing sugar on a cake, and had a package that his tight carefully tailored Armani slacks hugged like cling wrap does to beef in the freezer.

Wealth, adoration, and success stalked him. And so did I.

What attracted me and got me instantly hard was his incredible sculpted ass. Perfectly round cheeks, full but not flabby, encased tightly enough that you couldn't help but notice them, especially if you were behind him as, inevitably, I was. I could not compete with the fucker, either in looks, physique, or economic ability. I hated the bastard. I believed I had more reason than most.

I had wanted that molded ass from the moment Mitch, or Mitchell, as it proclaimed in gold lettering on his desk nameplate, walked through the company's front doors. And because of my preoccupation, no, let's call it my fixation with that ass, I knew something about it that the folks in the company didn't: that ass was available to just about any man with a cock. Except me. How did I know? I'd followed it at night to the sleazy dives it visited; I watched countless cum-encrusted cocks ram their way inside, imagining it was my cock servicing that very willing, very pliable asshole.

Now it was helpless in front of me. I ran a finger down the crack, gently pushing at the puckered hole. Mitch struggled, but that merely impaled him further.

He screamed, "Fuck off!"

The same scream that embarrassed me when I'd taken my turn at his anal portal one night at a sleaze venue he frequented when he'd turned to see who his latest top was to be. He recognized me from the office, even though he'd never given me so much as a backward glance there. "No, not you. Fuck off!" he shrieked. "Next!"

Perhaps I should explain how Mitch came to be at my mercy. Well, my obsession…there I've said it, and I don't feel any great sense of relief in my admission…caused my stocks at the firm to plummet. While Mitch was in ascendancy, I was very definitely in descendency. In fact, I suspected that the meeting called for 11a.m. Monday in the boardroom was to seal my dismissal.

I had, weeks earlier, in an attempt to ingratiate myself with upper management, suggested a weekend of company bonding at the Medieval Fair, a tacky theme park across the river in New Jersey. Families could dress in optional costume, play at imitation jousting, as well as indulge in other pursuits such as wenching, wooing, and eating copious amounts of baked and broiled meats in a draughty banquet hall. Later, they could sleep off the excesses of booze and bonhomie in bunkhouse accommodation, all included in the price of admission.

The total came to considerably less than the cost of the CEO's new Bentley.

Management had, of course, fled to the comfort of their own homes, family in tow, in the late afternoon of the first day. Once they disappeared, I could put my real plan into action. There was a possibility it would lead to my arrest and incarceration, but I was counting on the embarrassment factor working in my favor. Basically, I was past caring. With my dismissal imminent, I was unlikely to find another job in my area of expertise, so why not wreak revenge on my nemesis.

I had fabricated some small infraction of the theme park's quaint rules, convened a court of Mitch's equals, if there was such a thing, that I had stacked with people who disliked him or downright loathed his pretty tanned ass, thus ensuring he was sentenced to an hour in the stocks. They also decreed that he be stripped to his underwear for the duration. That decision met with enthusiastic applause from a few of his female colleagues who, after I locked him in, took the opportunity to grab a feel of his package, before whistling in appreciation. It was strictly against the rules of the theme park to lock anyone in the stocks but, hey, it was time to break a few rules, if not throw out the whole book.

As I walked away, leaving him at the mercy of the more brazen female staff members plus a couple of vengeful male members, so to speak, I heard him cursing me and threatening dire retribution. When I returned two hours later, it was nearly dark, with most of the employees already at the banquet hall getting pissed. Mitch was screaming. "Let me out of here, you bastard! I'll get you for this."

I waved the key in his face, swatting his ass cheeks so hard he yelled in pain. I yanked his Aussie Bum briefs to the ground and then shoved them in his mouth. Seeing him like this, my cock got hard.

Pulling my belt slowly through the loops of my trousers, I let Mitch see I was serious. When I'd finally extracted the length of leather, I doubled it over and smacked it against my open palm. The sound was worse than the sting. It was originally for show, but when Mitch laughed and snarled, "You wouldn't dare," I decided that I would.

Walking behind him, I caressed his firm, inviting cheeks before crashing the doubled belt down on his butt. He screamed, more in surprise than anything else. It left a vivid dark slash across his tanned skin. I raised the belt again and brought it down harder. The more he cried out to me to stop the more I kept at it, striking repeatedly at the source of my frustration, until his ass cheeks were pink and warm. I ran my hands across them as Mitch whimpered.

I squeezed out lube, rubbing it into the heat as a sort of salve then traced my fingers around his sphincter, teasing it before plunging in to the third knuckle.

Yes, he pretended not to like it, the hypocritical bastard, so I dropped my jeans over my hard-as-diamond erection, then rammed brutally into his forbidden ass, slamming his head more securely into the stocks. God, his asshole felt good. It was almost worth the trouble I was in. I would dream of an ass like this for the rest of my life. Tight, slippery, and smooth as the Thai silk shirts he wore to work. He clenched his muscles; he couldn't help himself; a natural reaction to having a cock wedged all the way inside him.

"You're enjoying this aren't you, slut boy?" I crowed.

He grunted his denial into his briefs.

Whether he was flexing his asshole to make me come faster to get it over with, or whether he was actually enjoying it, I didn't know and didn't care, except the former made revenge all the sweeter. I fucked him hard; wishing I could burst into his guts. A fucking that intense doesn't last long; all-too-quickly I spewed my load inside his ass.

I pulled out as we were joined by five guys in ski hoods. Yes, there were a few guys in the company who hated God's gift Mitch almost as much as me; a chance at his ass or his mouth was too good an opportunity to pass up no matter how straight they were. This had nothing to do with sexual satisfaction, although that was a given. This was about payback.

As the next guy lined up at Mitch's pliant ass, the rest of us set an old discarded wooden crate we'd found in front of him to make it easier to slip a cock into his gaping mouth. Now that Mitch could see that I was not his anal tormentor, he relaxed and I removed the gag. The hooded guys took turns at his asshole and his throat until their spunk dribbled from his well-used, gaping holes.

I took my place at his mouth. He shook his head violently. Holding his nose until he had to open up or suffocate, I slid my cock in until he gagged. I warned him of the consequences of biting me, and showed him the photographs we'd taken on our cell phones while he was in action, threatening to upload them to the net if he didn't cooperate, so he resigned himself to servicing me one more time. Grabbing the back of his head, I fucked his face, choking him, making him puke. I didn't care anymore and dumped my load in his mouth – I wanted him to taste me – then I pulled out. His look of triumph faded as he felt the first spray of my piss against his cheek. By the time I'd finished, his hair and face were soaked and his eyes scrunched closed as if they were stinging.

He spat as I unlocked the stocks, but he made no effort to get away. Instead, he turned to the anonymous gangbangers and shouted, "Come on, guys. Don't give up so easily. Fuck me again."

I had almost decided that Monday I'd stay home and they could fire me via email or text message on my cell phone, but I had personal items to pick up. There wasn't much to show for eight years with the same company, and they'd all fit easily in a cardboard box. I was watering the plant of unknown parentage that adjoined my desk and whose lush green leaves I had found friendly and soothing, when the summons arrived.

I couldn't escape, for Mitch, too, was in the boardroom for my execution. I prayed he would not get the satisfaction of pulling the lever. One of the senior partners, whether Kensington, Cletus or DeCoteau, I couldn't tell as they all looked interchangeable to me, cleared his throat and pointedly did not ask me to take a seat. Clearly, my stay would be a brief one.

"Mr. ...um..." He fumbled through his papers in an attempt to find my name, but gave up and just continued. "As you are well aware there has been a move to restructure this venerable old company, and no one has remained immune to its repercussions. We here at Kensington, Cletus and DeCoteau are indebted to the investment acumen of young Mr. ...um..." He shuffled his papers again until another of the senior partners leaned across and whispered in his ear. Mitch did not once lose his smile. "Um...Mr. Badham, that's right. He has been central to this company's astonishing, and I might add, unprecedented, growth. As a result, we will, this afternoon, be announcing to the media that Mr. Badham has accepted a partnership with the company. The youngest man ever to achieve this singular honor."

I wondered if it would be polite to puke at this point.

"However..."

Was I hearing this correctly? There was a 'however'? I looked at Mitch, and he was beaming. "There are a few tasks that, no matter how repugnant they may be, have to be undertaken for the smooth running of a company. Young Mr. Badham here suggested..."

Ah, this was going to be worse than I imagined.

"...has suggested a few improvements to take Kensington, Cletus and DeCoteau into the future..."

And by the looks on the faces of the old traditionalists, the suggestions had got up their collective noses, but Mitch had them over a barrel.

This was death by a thousand cuts.

"These are your ideas, Mr. Badham, so why don't you break the news."

When Mitch turned to me with that self-satisfied grin, I had taken enough punishment. In a voice that I hoped was not wavering too much, I interjected, "Why don't we stop the bullshit, gentlemen. We know why we're here. I've cleared out my desk and watered the hydrangea." It was the first plant I could think of, and I doubted upper management would have any more of a clue about its parentage than I did.

Mitch looked distressed. One point for me.

The senior partner looked bemused. "How could you possibly know? Mr. Badham has only just made known his demands...er, suggestions, and we have only this morning agreed to them."

Mitch was surprisingly placatory. "Perhaps Clayton..." at least he knew my name, although I hate it when people use your given name in an attempt to cushion the pain of bad news. "...Mr. Furst may have thought you had more sinister motives in calling him in today." The senior partners harrumphed which indicated to me that they did. "If you would give me time, gentlemen, I would be pleased..."

"Splendid," the senior partner said, standing before he got to the second syllable of the word. The boardroom cleared faster than an elevator after someone's farted. When the door closed, Mitch moved to the senior partner's chair, leaned back and put his feet on the table. That was sacrilege, albeit in extremely good taste, as his Berluti Rapiécés Reprisés shoes testified. He saw me register them.

"Sit down, Clay. No, up here next to me."

I could have walked out, but Mitch still made me hard. I'd thought that once I'd pounded his fuck hole I'd be over it. Not gonna happen. The more I looked at the malevolent young man, carelessly arrogant at the head of the boardroom table where he looked totally at home, the more I wanted to throw him down and fuck him.

He smiled as if reading my mind. "Why don't you then?"

'Why don't I what?"

"Throw me down on the table here and fuck me?"

"Because you'd probably enjoy it," I said.

"Why, Clayton. A compliment. That's the second you've paid me."

I was puzzled. "What was the first?"

"Going to all that trouble just to fuck me at the Fair."

"Yeah, I suppose it was." I had to smile.

"Was it worth it?"

"What do you want, Mitch?" I deliberately abbreviated his name because I knew he didn't like it.

"I'll let that one pass, for now. What do you think I want?"

"My balls on a platter. Preferably detached from my scrotum."

He laughed out loud. "Partly correct. Your balls would be great, but I prefer them attached, although like most men your age, you could do with some time at the gym, otherwise you'll go to flab. But that hair. Those clothes."

"I don't have an unlimited supply of cash. Right now I'm more concerned with how many weeks I can keep up my apartment with my rather meager savings."

"Oh, you don't have to worry about that. You won't. Keep the apartment, that is"

Callous bastard.

He pressed the intercom and spoke to the secretary outside. "Ms. Cresswell, Mitchell here. Yes, great news, isn't it? Thank you. Right, Valerie, could you get Security for me? Mr. Furst has left a box on his former desk. Could you please have Security collect it and put it on the desk in my outer office? No need for them to go through it. I will do that later."

"You won't find anything that isn't mine," I snapped.

"You disappoint me, Clay. I was hoping to find something incredibly incriminating. Whatever. It can always be planted there."

I had my hands around his throat before he could even blink. If he was afraid, he didn't show it. His face became more and more purple as I applied pressure, but he made no effort to call for help or even to fight me off. He just kept looking at me as if examining an insect under a microscope. It's difficult to throttle someone who remains seemingly indifferent to his fate. I let him go. Barely audibly, he gasped for air, straightening his tie. He took his feet off the boardroom table.

"You know you're a very attractive man, Clay."

That wasn't exactly what I expected him to say after what I'd just done.

"Yeah, right. You take every sleazy cock in that fuck hole you call an ass and reject me. I can see how that makes sense."

"I thought you liked my ass." He pouted, but it was a put on.

I sighed. "Truth be known I love your ass, Mitch. I loved every fuckin' moment I was inside you. I could fuck that ass all day and night and never get tired of it. I love standing behind you watching that little swish you've got. It drives me nuts."

"I think this has gone far enough," he said officiously. "Come."

Meekly I followed him from the boardroom, along the corridor to an office that bore his name in gold lettering, this time on an opaque glass door. He had informed the secretary stationed in the foyer that he was not to be disturbed under any circumstances, that included any one of the Messrs. Kensington, Cletus or DeCoteau in person or on the phone. She looked shocked, but gave him a conspiratorial smile.

There was something perversely compelling that made me complicit in my own execution. Normally, I would have just walked away, but Mitch was such the consummate game player, I had to see it through.

Once inside his outer office I whistled my appreciation. Not at the view, which was spectacular enough and revealed much more eloquently Mitch's worth to the firm than any press release, but at its sumptuousness and the presumption with which it had been furnished. If this was the office for his Personal Assistant then his own must be magnificent. Gone was the gloomy, nineteenth century wooden paneling and the fusty Dickensian bookcases, replaced with state-of-the-art plastics, chromes and glass.

On the walls were contemporary works by more than merely fashionable names. The decoration was ambitiously modern, but stylish with an air of longevity. On the corner of a desk embedded with computer screens lay my working life in a simple cardboard box. Maybe I was a dinosaur and it was time for the Mitch Badhams of the world to have a turn.

"You designed this?"

He nodded. "Every detail, right down to the color of the carpet and the artwork on the walls."

I whistled again.

"Come inside," he said and opened the door to his inner sanctum.

I was right; it was magnificent. Much like the outer office, but larger and more suited to a mogul. Sparse, but electronically astute. The art on the walls reflected it. Rather than paintings it was photographs. I noted three or four Mapplethorpes, and they weren't his flowers.

"Sit down, Clay," he commanded as he hung his coat in the spacious hidden closet.

His revenge was either going to be long or vicious if I needed to be seated for it. Or both.

He removed his tie as he leaned back against the desk in front of me. He pushed a sheet of snow white paper and a pen toward me.

"What's this for?" I hoped he wasn't expecting me to write out a confession.

"Just jot down the names of the men who fucked me while I was in the stocks."

"Kiss my ass!" I snapped.

"Why, Clayton, you're developing some balls."

He flipped the paper over to reveal half a dozen neatly typed names. My look of surprise gave the game away. I leaned in and crossed one out.

"Thank you, Clayton, that's all I need to know."

"Look," I stuttered. "I organized the whole thing. They had nothing to do with it. Sure, they took advantage of the situation but, hell, that ass of yours and that cute cocksucking mouth, who could resist?"

Mitch made a show of counting the names before, "I would say approximately the forty-three male members of the staff not on this list. Pun intended."

I sighed. "I'll sign anything you want, just leave these guys out of it. They have families, commitments."

"What an old softie you are, Clayton. Perhaps I wanted to know their names because I want a repeat performance. A couple of them were good. Very good, in fact."

My mind flashed back to the weekend and my cock snapped to attention.

He buzzed the secretary and asked that the five be in his office pronto. He then took his rightful place behind his desk and waited. There was no small talk, and I wanted out ASAP.

When the men arrived, they were the cream of the company. Mitch had them pull up the plush chairs that surrounded his throne.

"Now, gentlemen, I know that you were the five who fucked me at the Medieval Fair on the weekend." He held his hand up to stop the murmuring. "I'm hoping none of you will deny it because that would be most unfortunate for the furtherance of your career. No, Mr. Furst did not name names. I worked it out for myself from distinguishing marks, etc. You really should have blindfolded me, Clay."

There was a long pause while he gathered his thoughts. "Gentlemen," he began as he rose, "I fully intend to take control of this company within the decade."

"And take over the world by when?" one of them cut in sarcastically.

The rest laughed.

Mitch kept his temper. "I don't see any of you in an office like mine." The men sobered up very quickly indeed.

"You can come along with me for the ride. You'll find I'm very generous. In return I expect total obedience."

I wondered what the hell I was doing in the room.

"Unfortunately," he paused, "there is room for only one of you to inherit that office outside as my P.A. I have accepted a partnership on the condition I run my own show. How about it gentlemen?"

The men had relaxed since there had been no further mention of their weekend indiscretion. Until one of them asked," What do we have to do?"

"Ah," Mitch said. There was a world of possibility in that one sound.

"First up, as my good friend Clay was good enough to organize my gangbang, I thought we might pay him back with a similar little party."

I was up and at the door in seconds, but it did me no good as it was locked.

"I took the precaution when the last of your fellow workers arrived, Clay."

"Come on, guys," I begged. "Can't you see what he's doing?"

"What they can see, Clay, is that I'm offering them a rosy future." He turned to them. "Well, what are you waiting for?"

"You're serious?" Mark, one of the guys asked.

Mitch sneered. "Deadly."

"Count me out. Doing you was one thing," Mark said bravely. "You're an arrogant cunt, but I have no bitch against Clay."

"Pity. You're cute." Mitch leaned over the intercom and buzzed the secretary. "It's Mitchell here. Send Security to remove Mark...um...well, you'll see him outside my office shortly. Have Security escort him from the building. He no longer works here." He turned to the room. "Anyone else?" No one else volunteered. "Oh, and Mark. Going to the authorities will do you no good. I will have hackers laying a trail of deceit and malfeasances going back years in your computer before you even get home. It will remain our little secret for as long as you keep your mouth shut." After Mark left, snarling his hatred, Mitch closed and locked the door against further interruption.

"Now, gentlemen," he said to the others in the room as he removed his shirt and belt. I was manhandled, stripped, and forced to my knees. Mitch's trousers came down and he folded them neatly over his chair. Soon he was totally naked, and even in my situation I had to admire his body. He rippled with muscle; his cock brutally hard jutted smugly straight up along his stomach.

"I'll give you the opportunity to slick my cock with your mouth, Clay, because I seem to have left the lubrication at home. Dear me. So, any spit you manage to get on my cock will be of benefit when I fuck you. And no biting or you'll suffer the consequences."

He slid his cock into my mouth and down deep in my throat. I used every technique I knew to make it spit ready. Mitch slam banged into my gullet. As his breathing increased I tried to suck him to orgasm, but he wasn't going to fall for that.

"Gentlemen, put him on his back on my desk, if you please."

I was dragged into position and my legs splayed and pulled back over my head so my asshole was totally vulnerable. Mitch spat on my sphincter and invited the others to do the same. Then he rubbed it in with his finger, lining his cock head against my hole. This was gonna hurt.

Without warning, he pushed his way in. I was dry so the pain was hell. I tried to blot it out, but Mitch, smiling down at me, spat in my face. He leaned down and whispered in my ear. "Nobody fucks with me without my say so, Clay. You never were good enough for me and your feeble little revenge has come back to bite you on the ass. I'll fuckin' crush you and anyone who stands in my way. Don't you forget it."

He pounded my ass until I was on the verge of pleading for mercy, and then he shot his contempt inside me. "The first one to make him whimper gets the rest of the week off on full pay. Flip him over boys. I don't want you getting all sentimental looking at him. He's nobody. He's a worthless lump of meat with a hole, only good for fucking."

My face was pushed down into the desk and my asshole raised. The four of them took turns with ever increasing force although their cum helped lubricate my hole so it became less painful with each cock. I went inside myself and pretended I was enjoying the gang assault, that I was in control. I spun a fantasy around the predicament until my cock was convinced and got hard. I remained in this rainbow land of hard, married man cock pummeling my asshole until the last of them finished and I surfaced to reality. My asshole reeked of manjuice and throbbed with forced entry.

"No winners to my little competition, I see," Mitch said. He pushed a computer stick across the desk. "There's a cardboard box of Clay's meager possessions on the desk in the outer office. I need one of you to place this piece of evidence subtly enough that it will appear he has tried to hide it, but not so subtly that the morons in Security won't find it."

There was a general scramble with much pushing and wrestling, but I was too busy gingerly getting dressed to worry about the outcome. I was waiting patiently by the time Security arrived to find the evidence of my duplicity and escort me ignominiously from the premises.

The days and weeks that followed, as I sought new employment and a less pricey apartment, are now a blur, and it was only with the help and the strength of my few remaining friends that I pulled it together. That was three years ago. Now I have a successful career working for a charity that offers scholarships to underprivileged teenagers to attend university. We are able to do that because of my astute investment of donations.

It wasn't easy at first as some board members criticized my economic timidity, pointing to the large returns other charitable organizations were getting, particularly those with Kensington, Cletus, DeCoteau and Badham. They stopped complaining in 2008, when a number of financial firms went belly up with tens of thousands losing their money.

There was even a high-profile court case over insider trading and anomalies in one trading house. A partner of the firm whom many felt was the scapegoat for the whole rotten system, was sentenced to four years and eight months in jail. I've taken to driving the two hundred-odd miles to visit Mitch in prison. I'm his only visitor, but he's still full of grandiose plans for the future. He looks good. He's using the prison gym to keep his body in shape, but psychologically he's a mess.

Mitch has 438 days left to serve, with time off for good behavior. He's asked me to pick him up when he's released because he has mapped out a trajectory for the two of us that includes a suite in Trump Tower, me as his P.A. with fuck privileges, perhaps even some sort of permanent live-in arrangement. But I don't know. Sure, the memory of that sweet ass still haunts me, but one year, six months and five days seems such a long way off.

SCARFACE

"Fuck you, queer," he screamed at me, before doubling over in pain because I'd kneed him hard in the balls.

"So which one of your gang kissed and told," I said through gritted teeth. This might be Sydney in the roaring 1920s, but it was still against the law to bonk another bloke. And, you paid more dearly if you happened to be a member of one of the razor gangs that ruled the inner city streets. Make that ex-member. You could stick your cock in a goat, especially if you were a former Sicilian farm boy, and no one would turn a hair, but just try sticking that dick in another bloke, and you paid with banishment, humiliation and, occasionally, with your life. I wasn't sure which choice I was being offered, but I didn't like the odds: two against one, and they both had open cut-throat razors.

I'd tried wit to disarm the situation, but these two gang members had about as much appreciation of humor as genital lice, and were just as difficult to shake off. That's why my second approach had been more direct: a painful assault on the testicles.

I thought his agony would have given me time to escape, but his mate was already on me from behind, a position I sometimes enjoy, holding me securely for his injured partner who had balls of steel if his quick recovery was anything to go by.

I felt the razor slice down my cheek. I just had time to admire its intricately carved ivory handle before the blood flowed. It was a beauty, yet as brutal looking as the two bastards who had attacked me.

Don't get me wrong, I was no innocent, and my punishment was no more than I deserved if you lived by the law of the streets. Nobody, but nobody, goes behind the back of the razor gangs. I'd tried it on, and now I was getting my payback. My only hope was that my attackers were trying to scare me off rather than kill me. Mutilation would attract little attention, whereas a murder, well, that would have the cops out.

The pain would be swift and the blood copious. The wound I would wear with pride, and the scar would be my ticket to legitimacy, but it stung more than I expected, the blood spurting into my attacker's face and on his thug standard vest as well as his working class hat and trousers. He swore profusely.

The blood in my eyes blinded me, still I lashed out in an attempt to injure my bashers. There was a thud, like the sound of a nose breaking then another, this time sounding like teeth shattering, followed by a shower of curses. I knew I had not made contact so while I was waiting for the inevitable punch to floor me, I wiped the blood from my eyes with the sleeve of my shirt. My vision cleared just in time to see my two attackers high tailing it down the street with a woman in hot pursuit, wielding a lethal looking handbag.

Okay, there may have been a tinge of hysteria to my laughter, but I bent over double fit to piss my trousers. Clutching my sliced cheek to staunch the flow of blood, I just hoped the bastards were well seen fleeing the wrath of some woman and her handbag. Admittedly, she was a big cunt, but they would still never live it down.

Suddenly light-headed from shock or blood loss, I stumbled but felt strong arms grab for me to hold me up.

"Steady, love," she said. Her deep smoky voice made my balls tingle. "The bastards are gone, but they'll definitely be back. And with mates for back-up this time. I think two's me limit, love, so best if we get out of here quick smart."

"Thanks…um…love," I said ignoring the pain surging through my body. The attackers had managed a few well-aimed blows to my kidneys and my face, as well as slicing me open. I was no sissy, but I knew I was soon gonna hurt bad, real bad.

"Ruby. Ruby Red. Like the lipstick. A bit like your blood, in fact," she said. "Look, I live near here, why don't I get you home, and then we'll decide what to do next."

I was in no condition to argue. She was a prossie, it was obvious: make-up applied too thick, hair dyed just a little too brassy, and a dress that let you see from Sydney almost all the way to her map of Tasmania. I didn't care even as she shouldered me along the footpath shoving aside gawping bystanders to their utter consternation. Down the back streets of working-class Darlinghurst to Palmer Street, the unofficial red-light area in which women sat in various states of undress in their front doorways to lure prospective customers into their depressed, run-down cottages and terrace houses. We stopped outside a modest single storey dwelling in a side lane. She kicked the door sharply, and it flew open.

"Lock don't work, love," she said by way of explanation as she bundled me down the narrow hallway to the lounge room. I just had time to register that the building's dowdy exterior in no way reflected the warmth and, yeah, downright class of the interior before she dropped me onto the lounge and banged her fist against the wall, shared with the house next door.

"Timmy! Timmy! Get your flamin' arse in here now," she screamed. And, as if like magic, a few moments later a young man, obviously the Timmy she was hollering at, ran up the hallway. He was a slight lad, maybe twenty, ragged blond hair hanging over his pool blue eyes, with a smile so wide it seemed cramped in the room's interior. Until, that is, he clapped eyes on me, and he shuddered involuntarily. I guess I looked a mess.

"Timmy, go get doc and see if you can hurry him. Here," she said rooting around in a cupboard under the sink, "Give him this." She'd found a half of cheap brandy and was pouring most of it into a glass before handing him the dregs remaining in the bottle. "Tell doc if he hurries, there'll be more where that came from."

Timmy nodded, turning back to look at me again. "He's pretty," he said and then giggled at his provocative behavior before fleeing.

"Don't mind Timmy," she said, holding my face up by the chin to wipe the drying blood away with an old rag she'd dampened under the tap. Her fingers were gentle so I relaxed into their care.

"Is he any good?" I asked.

"The best," she said of the doctor. "Unless his hand is shaking from lack of grog. That's why I always keep a spare bottle handy. Without booze, he's a mess. With a bottle of gin or brandy, hell anything that's got alcohol in it, and he could operate on the king himself, and no one could do better. But there's gonna be a scar. A nasty one."

She cleared away most of the blood, stepping back to admire her handiwork. "Hmm, Timmy's right," she said. "You are a pretty one. The scar will add character."

She slipped to her knees, leaning up to kiss me on the lips. "Just got enough time, I think. Here, hold this cloth against your cheek, love." She began to unbutton my trousers. They were spattered with blood and street grime, but I didn't think her intention was to clean them. She had other things in mind as she made obvious when she clamped her hand around my cock.

I shuddered at the surprise of it. Sure, I was wary because she sported finger nails that could have gutted a chicken. "I haven't got the makings," I said.

"Love, I'm doing you for the sheer pleasure of it."

My cock was semi-stiff already just from the feel of her hand against my balls, and when she put her lips to my knob it sprang fully to life. She didn't waste any time, swallowing me right down to the root. I watched her scarlet mouth as she bobbed back up for air and left a snail trail of lipstick on me old feller. It was a real sight as she forced my dick down her throat without even gagging. I'd never had anyone do that before. Usually, I had to hold the back of their head, and then they'd spew. Ruby was a natural. She was doing things with her tongue that I'd never felt before…She lapped along my shaft as she was sucking my cock at the same time.

She must get a lot of return trade, I thought as I tried to hold off from her expert service.

"I don't think…" I said.

"I know, love. When you're ready," she said, taking her luscious mouth from my prick.

I arched my back, and she pushed her mouth back over my cock and down to my balls. I shot a load into her. Most pull away at that stage to spit out anything that gets in their mouth, and then handle you until you blow on the sheets or the footpath. Ruby swallowed every drop, swirling her tongue around my slit to siphon off the dregs.

The front door opened, and Timmy bounded into the room as I tucked my dick away and my benefactress wiped her mouth in an exaggerated gesture to show her satisfaction. The smile dried on Timmy's face. He turned and slammed back down the hallway.

The doctor appeared shortly after, puffing from the exertion of hurrying, it would be too fine a point to call it running, as he was portly and stank of liquor to the extent it would have been dangerous to strike a match near him.

"This him, Ruby?" he enquired, nodding in my direction.

"Yeah, doc. This is…" Ruby began. "Well, names can be dangerous to know sometimes. Let's just call him Pretty Boy."

The doctor looked at me closely. "Good choice," he agreed as he opened his satchel.

Usually I hated the name because people used it as a put down, but the way Ruby said it, even the way the doc said it, sounded good. The way Timmy said it made it extra special, spearing me in the groin.

I don't remember much after that. The pain or some injection the doc gave me and I was in and out of consciousness. I know at one stage I felt stitches before my hand was swatted away. I felt a cloth against my forehead that was cool and soothing. I heard strange piano music that seemed to come from the house itself. I recognized doc's face in my foggy brain, and Timmy, always Timmy, looking concerned, looking pleased, looking…I couldn't quite place that look. And, of course, there was Ruby and those amazing lips.

I woke up shivering with cold to discover a young man in my bed holding me. He was as warm as a blanket, so I snuggled closer and drifted back into sleep.

It was chooks cackling nearby, the sun pouring through the fancy gauze curtains that woke me. Then the cock crowed. I couldn't remember where I was. Everything was unfamiliar. Someone was holding my hand. I tugged it. A young man's face hovered over me. He was beaming from ear to ear.

"You're awake," he smiled. I wracked my brain for a name to go with the infectious grin. I tried to reclaim my hand. He let it go reluctantly.

"Tim?" I said groggily. "That's your name, isn't it?" I tried to sit up.

"Yeah." He seemed pleased that I remembered. "Most people call me Timmy. I like Tim better."

"Tell me, Tim." I tried to recollect what had happened to me. "Was it you that shared my bed? Kept me warm?"

"Yeah," he said. "You was delirious. Throwing the blankets orf, wanderin' around the room. Someone had to stop you from hurtin' yourself. Ruby couldn't do it, she has to work. I didn't mean nothing by it."

"I'm sure. Thanks." I smiled to reassure him. "Could you do me a favor?"

"Sure, anything," he said enthusiastically.

"Can you get me a mirror? I want to look at the damage."

Tim hesitated.

"What's the matter?" I asked.

"I don't think you should. You're not so pretty at the moment." He wasn't smiling now.

My hand shot up to my face. My cheek felt swollen and infected. The sudden movement hurt my ribs. I grimaced. Tim was at my side caressing my face but avoiding my wound. He swept the hair from my eyes with his fingers. "Nice hair," he said, sniffing it.

I liked Tim close to me: the smell of him, the touch of him. He was young and would be very handsome in a year or two once he lost his teenage puppiness and masculined up a notch or two. Right now, he was soft and eager to please. Life would toughen him up, or he wouldn't survive. Obviously the lad had been mollycoddled.

"Was that you playing the piano, Tim?"

He looked pleased but also slightly embarrassed as he nodded his head.

"I heard you. Even while I was unconscious, I heard you."

"That's what I want to be, Pretty Boy. I don't think I can call you that any more. Oh, I don't mean you're not still good looking or anything." He was getting more tongue-tied the longer he spoke. "It's just the scar makes you look tougher, meaner. I think I'll call you Scarface."

Scarface.

"Yeah, I like the sound of that. I'll wear the name and the scar as a badge of pride in who I am."

It might earn me some respect.

"What is it you want to be, Tim?"

"Nothing. It's silly." His coy response reinforced the fact his dream had obviously been laughed at once too often.

"Come on, you can tell me."

"A piano player."

He blurted it out as if it was a major confession, surprised by his own openness.

"I've never told anyone that before," he said, clearly pleased with himself. "Not even Ruby. I practise when she's not home. When I'm good enough I'm gonna get a job at one of them clubs like the Dance Academy in Commonwealth Street."

Despite its ritzy name, The School of Dance was a front for a queer club that sold illegal booze after six o'clock closing. It was one of the few places in the city where men could go to dance with men and women with women. It was regularly raided by the cops even though they were on the take. The sheila who ran the place, Black Aggie, was a friend of mine. I'd keep that snippet to myself for the time being.

"Any chance of some breakfast?" I asked to stop Tim's confessions from becoming too intimate.

"Coming right up," he said as he scooted out to the kitchen. I supposed that I reeked, but when I sniffed my armpits and other parts of my body, I seemed comparatively fresh.

"Did someone wash me while I was asleep?" I called.

Yeah, me and Ruby took it in turns. You were rank, Scarface. You don't honestly mind the name, do you?" He came to the door holding a heavy metal frying pan. "I can keep calling you Pretty Boy if you like. You sure are pretty all over," he said, and before the blush could color his entire body, he went back to the stove.

Relaxing into the soft mattress, I chuckled, wishing I never had to get up. But business called. I had to make my presence felt and mark out a territory if I was to survive. I had to pay back the bastards who cut me because the revenge had been Ruby's, and I had a personal score to settle.

I could smell bacon sizzling and my stomach did a somersault. "How long have I been here exactly?" I called. I heard Tim padding to the bedroom. "Three days," he informed me.

"I best be thinking about heading off then," I said.

His face fell. "No need to hurry."

We were interrupted by a loud knocking on the front door. It wasn't Ruby; she knew just the right spot to kick it open. The coppers would have announced their presence by beating the door with their truncheons in order to intimidate.

"Help me up, Tim."

"I can handle it," he said with surprising maturity, although I still doubted him.

He strode down the passageway and I heard the front door open. I heard him giggle then a number of brusque voices as men pushed their way inside. I was grateful for Tim's act, he'd perfected Timmy as a shield, and I realized he used it even with Ruby. Three men burst into the bedroom. I looked helpless lying on the bed. I might win the first skirmish, but I'd certainly lose the battle. My hope was to inflict some serious damage before I went down.

"Okay, queer," the front man yelled. "We don't like your kind. You give the rest of us a bad name."

"Is that why you line up to get your greasy cocks sucked when you think your mates are not looking?" I laughed.

He didn't take kindly to my sneer and I only just managed to duck his fist as I slammed my foot into his belly knocking him back into his bruiser mates. I flung off the blankets and was on my feet in record time. I slammed my foot down onto his windpipe. He gurgled and spluttered: it would be some time before he was back in the fray.

His mates closed in on me. I went for the nearest man and had the wind knocked out of me. I doubled over in pain.

One of them grabbed the front of my singlet to pound me to a pulp. I swung my head forward, connecting with his chin, and heard a loud crack, hoping it wasn't my skull but his jaw or at least some of his teeth. I was dizzy from the impact, still I saw the third man open his cut-throat razor. "We've been gentle on you so far," he growled. "That's over!"

There was no way in hell I could get near him while he was swinging the razor in my face.

The thwack to the back of his head must have woken the neighborhood, and he went down quickly. Tim stood triumphantly swinging the hot frying pan. Eggs and bacon and cooking fat splattered across the wall, but I didn't think Ruby would be too upset with this addition to her interior decoration. Anyway, I would pay to have it cleaned.

"Oh, Jesus," Tim was breathing heavily from the exertion, and his daring. "I'm so fucking stiff."

He dropped the pan, conveniently enough on the head of the man he had just whacked, and was on top of me before I could prevent it. He forced his tongue between my lips and into my mouth. I liked this Tim. My tongue went to meet his and they began to battle for dominance. I sucked his tongue gently before pushing it back into his own mouth and fucking mine into his juicy throat.

I felt between his legs. He was stiff. As stiff as I was. I heard a groan, remembering we had unfinished business. "Much as I want this to continue, Tim, we have something else to attend to first."

He nodded that he understood I wasn't rejecting his advances before heading off to find rope as well as cloth for gags and blindfolds. Tim knew of a safe house and we walked the men along dunny lanes and through backyards to disorient them so there would be no reprisals on those who were about to house the bastards.

Back at Ruby's, Tim looked at me expectantly.

"You're a brave bloke, Tim," I said.

He seemed to grow in stature at the compliment.

"Not like you, though," he said. Then he added shyly. "I like you, Scarface."

"I can see that," I said pointing to the bulge that was obvious in his trousers.

"I guess I can't hide what I am," he said.

"You shouldn't try," I replied.

"You knew Ruby was a bloke in a dress, didn't you?"

I laughed. "Of course, I did. Not what I usually go for, but she did me a favor, and it sure didn't hurt having her chow down on my cock."

"I was so jealous when I saw what she did to you."

"Then why don't you do it to me now" I encouraged by dropping my drawers to the floor.

He seemed surprised. "Are you like me, Scarface?"

There was a hesitation in his voice, as if he was worried I might take offence at the implication.

"One hundred and ten per cent," I said.

"But you could get any girl. You could pass," he said.

I just grabbed him, pushing him to his knees. Okay, his technique was not as good as Ruby's, she was a professional after all, but it was still fine. He played my cock like he played the piano: enthusiastically. He tugged its length before plunging his wet warm mouth down until his nose tickled my cock hair. I automatically placed my hand on the back of his head, but I had no need to force him. My cock fit his throat like a velvet glove fits a hand.

Tim moved tentatively to my arse and I felt him push against my hole. He looked at me to gauge my reaction. "It's okay, Tim. I go both ways." He smiled around my cock and almost choked. He doubled his efforts so successfully I was close to shooting a big juicy load into his mouth. I wondered if he swallowed like Ruby did.

I managed to groan that I was close, but he didn't, like so many others before him, take his mouth off my steamy cock and start tugging on it. I hate that. He sucked until I shot my juice into his greedy cocksucking mouth to dribble down the back of his throat. Ruby had taught him well.

"You got grease?" I asked.

He disappeared from the bedroom, returning with a jar of Ruby's cold cream. I was stiff and sore from the attack and wondered how I could keep my pain to a minimum. I dearly wanted to watch Tim's face as he fucked me but that would have to wait. I kneeled on the bed to let Tim grease my arsehole and loosen me up with those long elegant fingers of his. Two, then three, slid into my hole, and he pushed in and out to get me ready. My cock was stiff again as I felt him kneel behind me and press the tip of his cock against my hole. He pushed gently: a little too gently for my liking. I pushed back against his hardness, my arsehole stretching to swallow his prick down to his balls. I gritted my teeth until I got used to the initial pain and gave Tim the okay to give it to me by squeezing my muscles around his invading cock.

He felt good inside me, and he certainly knew what he was doing. I wondered how often his cock had been up Ruby's arse as a non-paying explorer. I groaned. Tim thought he was hurting me and slackened off.

"Don't fuckin' think, mate, because I take it up the arse I'm any less of a man like those bastards in the gangs do," I said.

"Stop your bloody yacking, you're throwing me orf." He pushed his cock into me at a different angle and bingo! It prodded something inside that made me see sparks. It also made me shoot again. My cock twitched and my arse muscles clamped around Tim's cock while my spunk slimed over the bed. Tim grunted, shooting his wad into my guts. He collapsed on top of me, panting, and I howled in pain.

"Sissy," he grinned, but lifted his weight off my battered body. I swatted his arse cheeks, and then ran my fingers along the crease till I found his warm hole.

"You want to be my punk?" I whispered.

"You mean it?" His eyes widened in incredulity. "Why would a tough guy like you want a fairy like me?"

"Maybe because you need a protector." He went to interrupt and I put my lips to his to stop him. "Could be as payment for looking after me so well. Or…it might even be that I like you."

He grinned, hugging me tightly until he realized he was hurting me then let go, apologizing profusely.

"You think you might like me? I can't believe it. I dream about you. Being with you. I never thought that could happen. Not in a million years."

"Calm down. I said I 'might' like you."

He nuzzled against me. "I'll help you make up your mind."

"You don't know anything about me."

"I don't need to. I know you're a very nice man. That you would never hurt me."

"I'm a nasty man, Tim. I hurt people for a living. And I aim to go on hurting people. Especially the bastards who pick on queers."

"What are you going to do with the blokes that came looking for you?"

"Trade them back to their gangs for a truce. Get back in with one of the groups."

"If you can't?"

"Don't worry yourself about things like that," I said, ruffling his hair.

"Don't treat me like a kid! I don't like it." Tim was fiery when angered.

"Sorry. All I meant was I might start up my own gang."

"A queer gang?"

I laughed at the very idea, but something took root.

"Not sure there are enough of us around to make up a whole gang."

"There's me," Tim volunteered. "And Ruby. And…" He rattled off a good dozen names, including a handful of male prossies who went out in dresses.

"I thought you wanted to play the piano?"

"Well, we all gotta have a dream, even if it's impossible," Tim replied.

Not that impossible if I have something to say about it. But that can wait.

He hesitated before he spoke again. "Where will you live?"

"I had a room but I guess I won't be welcome back there any more now that my reputation is in tatters."

"You can come and stay with me. I live next door on me own. Since me parents died. Ruby helps me out with what I don't understand an' everything."

It had its appeal. I'd be in the thick of it and it would help to have sympathetic neighbors.

He added hastily. "No strings attached."

"Don't you want me as your boyfriend, Tim?" I pretended to sulk.

"Are you serious?" he almost shouted. He went to lunge at me again but I moved quickly enough to avoid his clutches. "I always wanted a boyfriend. Ruby told me about queers who settle down like married couples."

"Hey, not so fast," I said trying to dampen his expectations a little. "We can try but there's a lot of rules to be worked out."

"All right. But I have a few rules of me own, you know."

"And what are they?"

"You have to treat me as equal, not some silly fairy boy. I insist on that."

He looked so serious I almost laughed. Almost. But I could see how important it was to him. Tim was stronger than I gave him credit for. If I wasn't careful I might even find myself falling for the bastard.

"I can do equals," I admitted.

"Do I get equal time with your arse?" he asked.

He was a cheeky little queer, but I'd never been one to associate masculinity exclusively with who puts their dick into whom.

"Any time, baby. Any time."

I wrapped my arm around him, grateful for the warmth, something in short supply in my line of business.

I had big plans, but for the moment I needed to get my strength back. It would take all the balls I could muster to put my plan into action, starting with the bastards that were trussed up like butchers' chickens. I'd make 'em shit bricks when I got my razor gang of queers together. I'd show 'em who the real sissies were.

'CEPS: MAD ABOUT MUSCLE

I admit it. I was foolish. I took a short cut down a laneway hemmed in on either side by the detritus of an artisan industrial heyday now long past. As the inner city became more gentrified and expensive, businesses had moved to the cheaper suburbs in the west leaving behind this enclave of single-story factories, mostly boarded up and empty, and yards crusty with ageing machinery.

The area wasn't considered dangerous but it was wise to avoid it at night because most of the street lights had failed years ago and never been replaced, the few that still flickered spasmodically merely reinforcing the eerie nature of the thoroughfare.

I hurried along the footpath, thankful for a moon which cast a silvery ghostlike light over the area. No sooner had I blessed the moon, than inky thunder clouds obliterated its light. In the sudden near darkness, I stumbled on the uneven footpath slabs, broken from years of neglect. Realizing I'd have to be more careful where I walked, I moved to the center of the narrow roadway, thereby avoiding the gaping doorways that could hide any lurking terror that my mind manufactured.

In the end, it didn't need to manufacture anything. I felt the stab of a sharp implement as it pierced my shirt and the skin on my back, followed by a warm, wet, rivulet of blood trickling down my spine. The voice was remarkably calm. "Don't make a sound, fucker, or I'll slice you open. You hear me?"

I nodded, then realizing it might be too dark for him to see my submission, I croaked an affirmative.

"Good boy," the voice soothed, before the knife, or whatever it was, prodded me toward a deserted yard protected by a rusting wire gate that proved no barrier to my assailant's boot. He was careful to always stand behind me so that I never saw his face.

"In there," he commanded, jabbing me again with the blade to get me moving.

I didn't hesitate. I had no intention of dying for the cash or cards in my wallet. I'd gladly give them to extricate myself from this situation. Robbery was my assumption, assault was my fear. He nudged me toward the back of the yard where even the wan light from the street didn't penetrate.

"Wallet," was all he needed to say. I handed it to him.

I never carried anything really precious, such as photos of loved ones or ATM numbers or computer passwords, but replacing the credit cards and ID cards would be a bugger. And there was close to five hundred dollars in cash. I hoped the thief was a drug addict who was looking for enough to buy his next stash. I dreaded being marched to the nearest cash machine, forced to reveal my security.

I heard shuffling behind me as my attacker obviously inspected his booty.

"This won't hurt a bit," the voice said as he wrapped his muscular arm around my neck.

I thought he was about to kill me by wrenching my head to the side suddenly. I tensed, fearing the worst, but not before I felt the warmth of his body against mine. He was a wall of muscle, obviously taller than me in order to loop his arm around my throat. It's funny what your brain chooses to concentrate on when you think you're about to die.

I felt the heat of his soft sausage-length cock pressed against my ass, I smelled sawdust overlaid with the heady fragrance of Old Spice, and, as the moon slid from behind cloud, I saw the band of barbed wire around the powerful bicep that gripped my throat. I heard him ask me something but it was all so hazy because I was gasping for breath, although I do remember the menace in his voice that made my prick hard. I remember answering in a croaky voice, and then everything went black.

When I regained consciousness it was light, just. I wasn't dead unless heaven or hell, or even limbo, is a junk-filled yard of weather-worn timber and busted electric saws adjoining a once stylish now dilapidated art deco brick building. The yard was hidden from the street by a large real estate sign stating the property was up for auction, giving the name and details of the real estate firm that was handling it.

I stumbled to my feet, still groggy, and wandered around in search of my wallet which I thought the thief may have discarded after taking the money and the cards. No luck. I also discovered my watch was missing. Okay, it wasn't a Rolex but it wasn't a piece of cheap shit either. He had left me my mobile phone, perhaps frightened that I had a tracking device attached. I did.

There was little activity in the street so there was no point in shouting for help. I didn't know what I would tell them anyway, so I rang the police to report the crime. As soon as they heard I was not injured, apart from the choke hold, and that I could not identify the culprit, they lost interest. I informed them I was reporting the theft for insurance purposes and insisted on a name and a reference number before I disconnected the phone. I didn't want details of the crime to go missing in action. There was too much at stake.

My secretary was next. After apologizing for waking her at such an early hour, I asked that she report the theft of the cards, to cancel them with the financial institutions, and to drive over and pick me up with a spare set of keys to my apartment. I wasn't concerned about his breaking in as I had all the latest high-tech gadgetry guarding the premises.

While I waited for Jessica to come and fetch me, I turned my attention to the forlorn office building. Cupping my hands to mask reflection, I peered through the dirt smeared glass. The interior seemed in good nick, the basic art deco ceiling, and walls untouched except for where someone had constructed offices. I searched through the vines and debris that partly hid the back door. A few swift kicks and it splintered, enabling me to force it open.

The ageing Venetian blinds that covered the front windows clattered from their housing when I attempted to yank them open for more light, disturbing the layer of dust that had settled over the floor and the remaining furnishings. I examined the floor, the walls, every little nook and cranny so that by the time Jessica arrived I instructed her to contact the agents to arrange for a building inspection. I intended following up my idea as soon as I'd showered and had a check-up with the doctor.

I'm very much of the school that believes the old cliché: every cloud has a silver lining. I'd lost my wallet and my watch, although 'lost' is probably not the right word to describe my mugging, but I'd found a derelict factory which seemed, on superficial examination, ideal for my purposes. I wouldn't let a little thing like an attack spoil it.

If I believed all I'd lost was a wallet containing some cash and cards, a watch, and consciousness, I was disabused of that fact when Jessica dropped me back home with the information my attacker had skimmed one thousand dollars from each of the three credit cards he'd stolen. The jumbled conversation that sat in my memory like stale frozen yoghurt must have been me revealing my ID numbers in exchange for my life.

Damn!

There was even worse when I discovered that high-tech gadgetry does not always prevent a determined thief from entering your premises. Yes, he'd found the spare cash I kept scattered around the various drawers and jars in my home. He'd also relieved me of expensive electrical and electronic products, although he'd spared my computer and laptop.

I gave silent thanks that he'd also spared me the pain that vandalizing the apartment would have caused. He'd left some pretty valuable paintings on the walls untouched, obviously not a connoisseur, and although he'd emptied drawers on the floor, there was comparatively little damage. I'd heard stories of thieves ransacking homes, especially those of the conspicuously wealthy, shitting their contempt on the furnishings and smearing it on the walls. Sure, I felt violated but a quick phone call to a security firm would fix that.

The police were more amenable to my call this time, sending around two members of the force to take details. They wanted to send a fingerprint expert but I'd seen what the white powder they used did to carpets and other household items, so I declined, telling them that I had insurance, and that all I wanted was an another official report to make a claim. Of course, I immediately fell under suspicion of executing the whole thing myself right down to the supposed mugging, especially as I had no physical scars from the attack.

A quiet call from my solicitor informing them of my net worth made an insurance scam of a few thousand dollars chicken feed. They backed off.

Within a matter of months, I managed to put the whole incident behind me. I bought the property, the location of my attack, and converted it into a two-story studio/office with living quarters upstairs. Although the street was industrial, the area was close enough to the city that young people were moving in, gentrifying the old terrace houses and turning factories into loft apartments. Within a few years, the street would be a haven for artists, gays, and bohemians. I was lucky to have bought before the property boom.

However, there was one aspect of the attack that I simply could not renovate. The man's smell and the feel of his body against me served as masturbatory fantasy for years. I imagined a face to the body, a rugged older man with jet black hair and raspy stubble, atop a body of pure muscle. Above all, it was the barbed bicep that rendered me unconscious that stuck in my mind like a faulty CD playing the same musical phrase over and over.

I started with an advantage, I was gay, so it wasn't like I had to change my gender attraction to accommodate a new fetish for biceps. However, I did join a gym, building up my own body sufficiently that I turned a few heads. It was no substitute for the dreams

I still had of that mighty muscle up tight against my throat. I began to pick up men with large biceps to role play my attacker and, while it brought momentary satisfaction, the incredible buzz was short lived.

It was almost embarrassing that my cock stirred whenever I saw a guy with his T-shirt bulging in the sleeve over his muscular arm: a workman on a building site, a lifesaver at the beach, or a young man with his girl. A number of times I looked up to discover the subject of my admiring gaze glaring belligerently at me, or was lucky to escape a bashing when my interest singled out one member of a group of men. I found a boyfriend, built large enough in the arms that he kept me satisfied for a couple of years, although he eventually tired of my charades, finally leaving me with the parting shot, "I can't compete with the man in your head."

Even therapy failed to alleviate the desire, mainly because, I freely admit it now, I didn't co-operate with the 'cure.' I rather liked the man in my imagination. He was infinitely more satisfying than the fallible flesh and blood I brought home from time to time.

Naturally enough, the police never pursued my case. They had nothing much to go on, and more important cases to solve. I understood that, even as I pressed them to find my attacker, although I never thought through what I would do once I had a name and a face to put to the man who tormented my dreams.

Then, unexpectedly, five years after the incident that changed my life, I did. I needed to clear my head for an important meeting that afternoon so walked the local streets, a solitary exercise I indulged from time to time. It relaxed my mood and my mind, stressed from too much concentration and computer work. I usually ended up in the local mall where I grabbed a coffee and Danish or a sandwich. This particular day, I headed into the supermarket to stock up on items that were running low in the small staff kitchen attached to my office.

I collected my purchases, daydreaming, not concentrating on anything much, including the queue in the '12 Items or Less' checkout aisle, when something assaulted my nostrils and sucker punched me wide awake. It was the sweet aroma of sawdust and Old Spice. I was instantly alert. Not one of the bored customers in front of me came close to fitting the hazy image I had of my real attacker. Then an arm reached past me toward a rack of chewing gum and breath fresheners the store kept to entice last minute impulse buys.

I froze. The aphrodisiacal scent pounded blood into my cock and to my brain. My pulse raced. He plucked a small tin of peppermints from the stand. I blew a load in my jeans the instant I saw the barbed wire tattoo that snaked around his bicep, much more powerful than I remembered it.

My body juddered as my spunk filled my pants, a small squeak of excitement escaped my lips and was thankfully lost in the clatter of voices combined with Muzak and precision-spaced bleeps from the adjacent barcode readers. I didn't dare turn around, fearful I would be disappointed, that the whole edifice I had created would crumble. I'd often imagined this moment. Well, not exactly as it had happened, but our meeting. It had to be him. The aroma was too distinctive, as was the band around his bicep.

I wasn't about to dial the police to have him arrested. They would probably laugh at me and my method of identifying my attacker. There was the minute possibility I could be wrong, although I doubted it. I passed through the checkout, spending more time than necessary bagging my small number of purchases. I heard him speak, his voice deep and resonant. It was *his* voice. The commanding tones that had demanded my wallet all those years ago. I liked it. It made my cock stiffen all over again.

Still, I didn't look. I pretended to be engrossed with the notice board at the front of the store until I saw him pass out of the corner of my eye. I followed, unsure what to do. I couldn't bowl up to him and accuse him of theft. That was a one-way ticket to a beating because the fucker was big. Not so much big as in height but big as in muscular. He'd snap me like a twig.

I was pleased to see his hair was jet black, spiky as if he'd merely run his hand through it casually. He wore a black singlet, the garb of choice of manual workers, which revealed a bushy growth sprouting from under his arms, a wide back, his arms bare, the ink on one of them drawing attention to the mouth-watering bicep. He wore tradesmen's shorts, dirty with scuff marks and grease, plus thick woolen socks that he rolled down over the tops of his sturdy work boots. He was a walking wet dream – from the back. There was a hint of stubble from the little I could see of his jaw.

Careful not to appear I was following him, I prayed he wouldn't turn around and dash my fantasy while also praying that he would so I could bury my fantasy once and for all. I panicked when I realized that my life would never be the same once I saw his face. It wasn't like I could ever have this man. Or ever get revenge. Or could I?

At that moment if I could have tasered him, I would have. But it was broad daylight in a crowded mall car park so my options were limited. I couldn't even follow him to find out where he worked or where he lived. By the time I ran back to my office to fetch my car, he'd be gone.

Luck, fortunately, was with me.

I heard the beep of the security from his key tag as he unlocked the door of his vehicle, a small truck that had the name of a company emblazoned across the driver's door. Retrieving my mobile phone, I captured a pic of it, and entered the phone number in my electronic guest book. I caught the merest glimpse of him at the wheel as he drove to the exit of the car park. It didn't disappoint but nor was it sufficient to supplant the image that dominated my mind. Let's just say, it blurred the edges a little.

Back at my studio, I closed the door to my office in order to clean up the mess I'd made in my jeans and then, hands trembling, I dialed the number from the truck door.

I managed to keep the nerves out of my voice, sounding thoroughly professional as I lied that the company had been recommended by a friend whose fictitious first name I dropped in the hope they would not ask for a last name. I was deliriously vague about losing the name of the worker who my friend had particularly recommended, and I couldn't ask him because he was currently overseas on business. I had been introduced to the workman I wished to employ and managed a sufficiently generic description.

"That could fit any number of our workmen," a helpful young secretary answered. "Any distinguishing characteristics? If not, I'm sure any one of our employees would be more than satisfactory."

She was in danger of going into full sales spiel. Somewhat rudely, I interrupted as if I'd a sudden brainwave. "Oh, I remember, he had a tattoo on his arm. Let me think, it was very distinctive. I know, it was barbed wire."

"Oh, you mean, Clint."

"Yes, that was the name. Clint."

I liked it. It was a man's man name. Rugged. Individual. Mugger. I had to control myself this close to my quarry.

It seems Clint was one of the company's more hardworking tradesmen and I would have to wait a fortnight before he was available. Not a problem, I assured the helpful young woman as I scheduled an appointment, failing to add that it would give me just enough time to prepare for what I had in mind.

I gave my small staff the appointed day off on the pretext of the extra work they had put into a particularly important contract and they accepted my largesse gratefully. So, when Clint pulled up in the yard, I was alone in the studio. I pretended to be busy in the foyer area when he pushed open the front door. My breath caught in my throat. Fantasy nothing; this guy was heaven on a stick. I'd already seen the ripped body from the back. It was more impressive from the front, his chest forming a plateau which his singlet hugged like an ardent admirer, his abs clearly outlined through the fabric. His looks were even more impressive; from the hair which I'd seen from the back through his piercing blue eyes to his square stubbled jaw and powerful chin.

"Can I help you?" I choked.

"I'm after a…" He hesitated while he consulted the card he had in his hand. "Scott Allen."

"That would be me," I said. "It's the staff's day off, so I'm being my own secretary today. Come in."

I ushered him through to my office, watching as he looked around the premises, whistling in admiration. "I wouldn't recognize the place," he said.

"You've been here before?"

"You probably won't believe this, but I used to own this factory and this land. Five or six years ago it was. Had a nice little set-up."

"Coffee?"

As I got his request and made one for myself, I asked him why he'd given it up.

"No choice, mate," he said without rancor. "My partner embezzled the business, bankrupted me. Bastard ran out on me. Took my missus with him."

"That's tough," I commiserated.

"They took everything. My business, my home, my truck, left me with just the tools I work with. And the shirt on my back."

I wasn't sure if 'they' were the partner and his wife or the trustees who oversaw the bankruptcy.

"You obviously made it," I suggested.

"Thanks to a guardian angel," he said, opening up. "I don't mind admitting I was here packing up wondering where I was going to spend the night. I had no home, no money, and I had to be out by morning. Then some money fell into my lap. It was like a miracle. It was enough to get me by for a couple of weeks. Get back on my feet. Start all over again."

"What, a win on the horses or something?"

"Let's just say 'or something' and leave it at that." He seemed uncomfortable now, as if he'd revealed too much. "What is it you need doing around here? Place looks pretty good to me. Must be worth a penny or two these days."

He stood to follow me outside but stumbled, gripping the edge of my desk for support.

"Whoa," he said. "What was in that coffee?"

"The usual," I said, as he followed me out into the back courtyard, stumbling drunkenly, trying to make sense of his clumsiness. "Coffee, milk, sugar, and of course…" I mentioned a strong drug often used by date rapists.

I saw the startled look on his face as he pitched forward and he would have landed face down on the paving if I hadn't caught him. He was a heavy fucker but I was strong enough to drag his body into the 'workshop' I had specially prepared for him. I secured his ankles and his wrists, leaving him to sleep it off. He'd be out for a few hours so I went back to my office after I'd cut his clothes from his body, leaving him sprawled naked on the tiled floor.

He was a delicious sight, good enough to lick all over. I restrained myself even as my cock demanded attention. I ignored it, concentrating on business, fielding a few phone calls, writing a few reports, generally keeping my mind occupied until I heard a shout from the workshop. None of the neighbors could hear him as I'd soundproofed the premises. I heard him because I left the interconnecting door ajar. There was panic in his voice. Good. He could stew for a while longer.

In fact, it was a good half hour before I walked in on him struggling against his shackles.

"You thirsty?" I asked.

"What the fuck?" he shouted.

I took that as a 'yes' and tossed a bottle of water to him. It landed perilously close to his balls. Glaring at me he none the less guzzled the water until he'd drained it.

"Let me out of this, you fuckin' cunt," he swore. "I'll fuckin' kill you when I get free."

Sitting myself on the floor well out of his reach, I replied calmly, "See, there's your problem. On the one hand you want me to let you go, then on the other you threaten to kill me as soon as you're free."

He understood immediately. "You let me go now and I'll walk out of here and I won't report this to the police or anyone. You have my word."

"I will let you go," I assured him. "But it will be in my own good time. I mean you no harm. I have no intention of killing you. Unless you make it necessary. If you do as I say, I'll release you. You might even have some fun."

He looked at me suspiciously. "What sort of fun?" He must have realized he was naked and closed his legs to hide his cock.

"You've guessed correctly,' I smiled.

"I don't do that shit," he spat.

"That is a pity," I said. I stood and pressed a button, starting the machinery that wound the chains restraining him tighter so that he had to stand, arms and legs akimbo, giving me total access to his body.

"Why are you doing this?" he begged.

I ran my finger down his chest and across his stomach to just above his cock. It bobbed briefly as my fingers approached, but I stopped before I reached it.

"Let me tell you a little story. I think you'll enjoy it. The synchronicity of it. It was one night about five years back. I was tired, in a hurry to get home. Normally I avoid the back streets but this night I decided to chance it because a storm was brewing. I cut down a laneway not so very different to this one." I pointed to the roadway outside. His look of confusion meant he hadn't picked up on the significance as yet. "I had no reason to suspect anyone lay in wait, but as I passed a deserted factory, not unlike this one in fact, someone grabbed me from behind and dragged me into the yard."

"So?" he snarled.

"You see, I never got a look at my assailant. He relieved me of my wallet, the keys to my apartment, and several thousand dollars. Plus a few other miscellaneous items. Ring a bell yet?"

He sounded less sure. "Why should it?"

"The man who mugged me left me unconscious while he raided my bank accounts, withdrawing the maximum amount, and stealing a few items of no importance to me. They were all insured."

He tried bluffing. "If you didn't see him…"

"I didn't need to," I continued. "You see, the guy had a distinctive smell. His deodorant or his cologne mixed with the smell of sawdust. You're a carpenter, Clint. You use Old Spice."

He was defiant. "That means fuck all."

"I agree." I walked around him, running my fingers lightly over his body which was doing things to his cock even though he seemed in fear for his safety. "But he made one mistake. When he wrapped his arm around my throat to choke me, and render me unconscious, well, something gave him away."

Clint's eyes went straight to his tattoo. "Shit!"

"As you say, Clint. Shit."

"Look, mate, you know the story. I didn't mean you any harm. Let me outa here and I'll pay you back every penny. I swear."

"I don't need your money. In fact, you did me a favor. I found this factory and bought it thanks to you."

"Making money from my misery."

"Don't try playing the victim, Clint. It doesn't suit you."

I slapped his ass hard, leaving a hand print on his butt cheek.

"So, if you don't want the money, just call the cops and I'll make a full confession."

"What? So they can haul you before the courts, if they even bother, where you'll get a slap on the wrist and a suspended sentence? I don't think so."

"Then what the fuck do you want?"

"Simple," I said. "Revenge."

"What the fuck?"

"The revenge can be as painful or as pleasurable as you make it. But I guarantee it will be pleasurable for me."

"Come on, man, let me go. I'm sure we can work something out."

"Just as you didn't give me a choice the night you attacked me, I'm giving you no choice tonight. Understand? I'll do exactly what I intend doing, and you can go along with it, or not. You'll be here until I consider

I've got full value for everything you stole from me and the fear you put me through."

I was behind him now. He was totally unprepared as the leather paddle swatted his ass. He cried out in pain. I followed quickly, smacking his other butt cheek. I alternated, reversed, changed my rhythm, everything to throw off his anticipation, prolonging the exquisite agony, until his cheeks were red and probably tingling.

"Feel free to scream as loudly as you like, no one will hear you. The room is soundproofed."

"You cunt, I'll get you for this."

"I might add that threats will do you more harm than good. If you try anything like that then you'll perish in here. The doors are locked, I have the security combination in my head, and you are trapped until I allow you to leave. No one will come looking for you because I have already sent an email to your company saying you didn't arrive here. I've also taken the precaution of removing your truck."

He must have believed his punishment was a beating because he snapped, "Okay, get on with it then."

"I should add that just in case anything should happen to me, there is an email programmed to send to my secretary at noon tomorrow detailing your original attack on me all those years ago including the police reference numbers so they can track it down and a neat little story about how you recognized me in the supermarket. The receptionist at your place of employment may contradict the story but with my influence it will be me they believe."

"You think you're so fuckin' smart covering all the bases. You smart cunts with all daddy's money, never worked a day in your lives. Don't know what real work is. Treat us like shit, trample all over the workers."

"Spare me the downtrodden worker bullshit. You don't know where my money comes from or how I treat my staff. But, if you hang around long enough, you might learn."

"Not interested. Get on with it or let me go. Clocks ticking. Time is money."

"How right you are."

Giving his ass a few lazy slaps, I grabbed two nasty clamps and moved to his chest.

I suspected he might try to head butt me. "Try it and I'll cut your balls off," I smiled.

My warning had the desired effect. I licked his nipples, sucking them into my mouth one at a time, nipping them with my teeth.

"So, you're a faggot?"

"Not a word I like." To reinforce the point I opened the teeth of the clamp and snapped one on his now erect nipple. He cried out in pain as it bit into his sensitive flesh. His agony did not prevent me from doing the same to his other nipple. He squirmed in his chains, his pendulous cock slapping against his thighs. Clint was uncircumcised, his balls and prick in proportion to the remainder of his body: big. It was going to be difficult to take my time.

He grimaced as I palmed his testicles, squeezing them harder than was comfortable, but I didn't want to bruise them, as I had other uses in mind. I slipped a leather cock ring around his cock and balls, snapping it closed before his cock was too engorged with blood. He grimaced as I ran a finger along the top of his shaft, watching it flex at my touch.

"Why don't you just get on with it?" he jeered. "If you're gonna fuck me, just do it, and let me go."

I merely smiled. "I don't really think you're the one giving the orders around here."

Sniffing his arm pits, I ran my tongue into the warm salty nook, licking his sweat, chewing the damp hairs, sucking his flavor into my hungry mouth. I ran my lips along his arm until I reached his magnificent bicep. I couldn't control myself any longer, kissing, licking, sucking that huge muscle as if it were the most delicious cock in the world.

Clint snickered. "You like my muscles, eh? Why don't you let me down and I'll pose for you. Give you a bodybuilder show. I done some stripper work, I know what the audience wants."

I ignored him, working over his other pit until it was spit clean. I ran my lips across his perfect stomach down to his trimmed pubes. Yeah, I suspect he still had a sideline as a party stripper. I wish I could see him in action but there was no way I was letting him down until I'd finished. The guy deserved the punishment I had lined up.

Just as he thought I was about to engulf his cock in my mouth, it stiffening in anticipation even if his hetero mind wasn't up for it, I ducked behind him. His whole body tensed. He made one last plea to save his skin. "You can fuck me if you let me down. I won't try to escape or anything like that. Just let me down and you can do me."

I was amused. "What makes you think a quick poke at your ass is worth all those thousands of dollars you stole from me? You must think you're pretty amazing stuff."

"Well, my ass is virgin. Never had a cock up there. So it'll be tight, right?"

"Virgins are so boring. Clenching their teeth, crying about how much it hurts, all that shit. Nah, if anything your virgin ass is worth less to me. To make up for my losses I'd need to keep you greased up and ready for a couple of weeks, if not years."

"Why don't you just call the cops? I'll confess everything. Then you'll have your satisfaction."

"I've had five years to plan my revenge and it won't be pretty."

I sounded tough, even to myself. But I had no real idea of what I was going to do. My anger had dissipated. I had a hot man strung up, if not by the balls, at least so that his very pretty balls were easy pickings. Yeah, I could have my way with him, but that would probably leave me feeling lousy and I wouldn't get the satisfaction I craved.

It didn't help that underneath it all, Clint seemed like a decent enough bloke who had run into a bad patch and, unfortunately, I'd stumbled across his path when he was desperate. Fuck it, when was it my turn? Deciding the answer was 'Now', I shucked off my clothes, standing in front of Clint totally naked, massaging my swollen cock. It felt so good to see fear in his eyes.

I needed some sort of closure. In frustration, I whacked his reddened butt with my hand then soothed it with a caress, gently fingering his crack. I wasn't interested in taking his virginity, but I was interested in that marble muscled bubble butt. I prized his cheeks apart, running my fingers down the moist crevice, across his humid hole, right on down to his balls. Clint shuddered, whether with pleasure or in anticipation of his deflowering, I wasn't sure.

Kneeling behind him, I buried my face between his spicy mounds, licking up and down until I'd tasted his funky sweat, before burrowing my tongue into his sphincter tunnel. It felt so good, my cock came close to spewing a load over the back of his leg. I thought I heard Clint moan.

"You like that?" I ventured to ask.

His voice cracked. "Never felt anything like it."

That spurred me on to a greater effort, licking and tongue fucking his tender asshole. He was too tense. I swatted him again.

"Relax," I said. "I'm not going to fuck you. You'll walk away with your anal cherry."

His relief was so great, his body sagged against his restraints, my tongue worming its way into his guts he was so pliable. His groans were now more voluble, encouraging me to further effort. I would have loved to free him but while he was defenseless, he could justify being 'forced' into such a sexual situation. Give him his freedom and he would have to choose whether to stay or go. No, better to keep him trussed up, for the moment anyway.

I slicked his asshole but my main target lay elsewhere. I had to have it. I shifted to kneel like a supplicant in front of his drooling prick, standing proud from his couture pubes. I snuffled his balls, drawing the scent deep into my lungs, then ran my tongue across the wrinkled sack before heading for the prize. It was the lightest of touches as I dragged the tip of my tongue along the underside of his shaft until I reached the glans. I swirled my tongue around the head of his cock like a vine around a stake, drawing it slowly into the warm slickness of my mouth.

His body bucked as I licked the drool from his slit, using it to lubricate his thickness. His cock was true art: long and thick enough to give me pause as to whether I could take it all. I would – or else choke trying. However, I was in no hurry as I slid my lips down the shaft so slowly and sinuously that he was desperately trying to force his cock deep into my throat, but the chains prevented him from achieving his designs, frustrating him.

"Come on, man. Suck it. Don't leave me in suspense."

"Maybe I should," I said. "It's probably what you deserve."

"Take pity on me, man. You suck better than anyone I ever had."

"And I've hardly started," I boasted. Then thinking about it, I added, "You've done this before, haven't you?"

He was coy. "Might have."

I chuckled. "Definitely have. Those parties you strip at: they're gay aren't they?"

"Yeah, some of them," he admitted. "Guys tip better."

"And blow you better, too, I bet."

"Maybe."

If this was an act, he was remarkably good, but for the moment, I wanted to remain in charge. My revenge wasn't half as punishing for him as I'd expected. In fact, it was hardly punishment at all. Clint was enjoying it, obviously having enjoyed a man's mouth around his cock on numerous occasions before.

I shrugged. Who gives a fuck!

I swallowed him right down to his balls, opening my throat so I wouldn't gag.

"Holy mother of god," he squirmed. "No one has ever taken me that far in one swallow. Shit, you're good."

I thought a response from me was the last thing he required, especially as he hadn't asked a question, so I continued to swallow, massaging his weapon with my throat muscles. He thrashed, he cursed, he bucked as my mouth made passionate love to his prick, bringing him to the edge and then letting him subside cruelly without relief. I didn't want to drive him over that edge just yet.

I kept it up for a good ten minutes. That may not seem like long but when you have a cock lodged in your throat it can seem an eternity. I wanted it to last, I really did, but in the end, both of us needed to unload. I buried my face in his pubes, tickling him with my tongue, encouraging him to spurt with my throat muscles, while I jerked my own cock. It was a competition to see who would come first. In the end, it was him. His juice shot down my throat unsavored, until I pulled back and the last of his spunk filled my mouth so I could taste him. A few seconds later, I blew a load over his foot and against his leg.

He hung limply, exhausted, the chains biting into his hands as he drew breath, before straightening himself to his full height, austere and demanding, stating baldly, "I think you should clean that up."

The power shifted. Even though he was in chains, he was suddenly in command, and I immediately kneeled to run my tongue down his muscular leg and across his foot to his toes, slurping up my own sperm. I was so excited my cock hardened again, something I had never managed so quickly after shooting a load before. I looked up at him subserviently, opening my mouth to show him the cum puddling in my mouth.

"Good boy," he said, and I knew he would have patted my head had his hands been free.

"Now, let me out of these restraints," he said with quiet command.

I knew it would all be over once he was free and although I was sated sexually, I was disappointed there was no more. Sure, I could keep him captive a while longer but why prolong my own agony as well as his. There was the possibility he would turn violent, but I doubted it. In the event, I was wrong.

I removed the nipple clamps and he grimaced at the cutting pain as the blood flowed again, and then I let him out of the chains. He pounced. I shouldn't have turned my back on him, I suppose. It was just like last time. He had his massive bicep around my throat, strangling me. Major difference this time – he was hard. So was I.

"Right, fucker," he breathed into my ear. "We'll see who's boss now."

I wanted to melt into his arms, to worship that muscle cutting off the air to my throat. If I was going to die, this was the way to do it. I thrust my ass back against his groin.

"Don't worry," he snickered. "I know what you need." So saying, he thrust his fingers between my ass cheeks and found my hole. He must have spit slicked his fingers because they slipped in comparatively easily.

"You've had men inside you before," he said. "I like that."

He thrust without care for my wellbeing and I felt his knuckles part my sphincter. It was rough, it was painful, it was fuckin' amazing. My tongue snaked out of my mouth to lick his bicep. I had nothing to lose now.

"I can help you," he said, withdrawing his fingers. I heard him spit in his hand, then his cock head poked at my entrance. With one almighty shove, he buried himself inside me.

My scream of pain filled the small room. He obviously meant to hurt me. I took deep breaths, concentrating on that love muscle choking me, knowing that shortly the pain would turn to pleasure. He was kind enough to give me a chance to relax but not enough that the first few breaches didn't hurt. As he picked up pace, though, I was so in tune with him I let go and pushed back driving him farther into my ass. Mewling sounds emanated from my throat, giving away my pleasure.

"You like my muscles, eh?"

"Uh huh," I managed to garble.

"I love someone who wants to worship my muscles. That gets me so horny. Doesn't matter to me whether it's a man or a woman. You like Clint's muscles, Clint likes you."

"I love your muscles. I want to get down on my knees and run my tongue over your entire body. Eat your hot ass, suck your pecs till they're hard as marble, rub my ass pussy against your biceps."

"Wow, man, you really get off on it, don't you?"

By way of reply, I put my mouth around his biceps and licked and sucked and moaned like a posh whore.

Grinding my ass back against his invading prick, I tried to suck him inside my body to show him just how much I wanted him. In return, he fucked me like I was a piece of human trash. That's what I'd been looking for all these years. Someone to use me, to use my holes. This man was a fantasy come to life. I relaxed into the fulfillment of a dream.

"Take it you fuckin' cunt," he spat as he pushed into me so hard I thought I'd fall, but his powerful arms were holding me tight. I wished he would never let me go.

I shot another load, the pulse of my ass contracting around his cock sucking the last resistance out of him. He spewed his load inside me, grunting as each squirt shot into my guts.

Then all was quiet, the enormity of what had transpired lying between us like a ticking bomb that neither wanted to disturb. His cock deflated, popping out of my ass, bringing us back to our situation. He could still beat the living crap out of me, or acknowledge his debt paid in full. Instead, he picked me up in his arms and gazed into my eyes.

"You're a scrappy little thing, aren't you?" he said, but he meant no malice.

"I could whup your ass any time," I boasted.

He laughed so much I was frightened he would drop me.

Then his face came over all serious. "That was a down payment for what I owe you. Okay?"

Not daring to speak, I shook my head.

"Not sure I remember what I took and what it was worth, but I'm sure you do. So, you calculate how much what we just did was worth and deduct it from the total."

"Okay," I said, hoping.

"I'll work off my debt to you that way. As long as you're agreeable," he said.

I wasn't sure I wanted a commercial arrangement. I was looking for something more, well, loving.

But still, I was quick to confirm, "Oh, I'm agreeable, all right. But it may take weeks, even months to pay off the whole debt."

Then he confirmed my dreams.

"Maybe even years," he said, as he slid his hand under my butt to finger my ass.

THE PLUMBERS' MATE

I was having a cunt of a day. No, make that a cunt of a week. I'd just had twenty-four of my books banned, Claudine my publisher at Perverts Ink was on my back because I was three weeks behind deadline for handing in my latest novel, and Bettany my editor had just emailed a set of new rules for avoiding objectionable matter in my writing only for me to note that my works did not breach a single one of them. What was going on? It was my idiosyncratic vanilla fiction excluding those very same objectionable subjects that made me a modest best seller, flying in the face of the more graphic and unseemly fiction of my sister and brother writers. I knew these new rules were not aimed at me but at the utter sleazebags who persisted in including profanities in their titles or introducing fisting or double penetration or... forgive me for not going on.

What the fuck was I supposed to write about? Flower show sodomy? Mother's Day ménage? Gangbangs in the garage? Oops, scrub them. Sodomy, ménage and gangbang, consensual or otherwise, were now all verboten. Seems I wasn't even allowed to have a pet dog in a story unless it was always twenty feet or more away from a human, in case readers suspected there might be a bit of cross-species how's-your-father going on.

Please note that I am not a hypocrite. Profanity in the privacy of your own home or your own mind is permissible but, really, no one wants to see it in print. Or at the movies. Do they?

If I ground my teeth any more I'd be down to my gums. I'd spent the best part of three days being totally unproductive, dealing with the fallout of the ban put in place by the near monopolistic financial monolith that is CashCow. The multinational corporation had originally been set up to make paying for items on eJunk that much easier but, like Topsy, it had 'growed' until now it was so ubiquitous it could dictate morality, wielding the big stick of disconnection if its demands weren't followed.

CashCow had found a niche and plugged it, so now we were all fucked. If you channeled your money through them you didn't have to pass on your credit card details to third parties. It was an easy way for small business, like my publisher, to set up a payment system that was comparatively painless to the people at either end of the deal.

Now, they'd issued a 'directive' informing small business what was permissible and what was not. Overnight, panic swept through the eBook market, in particular that genre known as erotica. That's where I come in. That's what I write: erotica.

Just to get it clear, we're talking erotica rather than porn. There is a fine line admittedly between the two but I like to think of erotica as the difference between good sex and a quickie. Erotica has characterization and tension, winding you up until your body screams for sexual release. Porn is like sticking your dick in a glory hole and hoping someone is on the other side to take care of you. One describes the mood, the furniture, and where it's all taking place; the other just tells you how big the cock is.

Not that I'm averse to describing a nice juicy dick or five. And I've described literally hundreds of them in my novels and short stories under various names, including my own, Tim Marsden. Tim writes vanilla gay erotica that usually ends with the happy monogamous couple riding off into the sunset together. Very popular with female readers. Sometimes I'm Luke Dark: vampire erotica. Sometimes Daisy Chayne: young adult fiction whose *Pansy Prufrock and the Fairies* is a favorite among eight to ten year old girls. Other times Pussy Tussle: lesbian ménage. That day I was Cindy Ginger: heterosexual romance with a touch of spice.

Except Cindy's ideas weren't coming. No one was coming, not even me. Sometimes I get so excited churning out my few thousand words a day that I have to leave off in the middle of an exciting passage to take myself in hand. That day the computer screen was blank.

I hadn't even entered the title or Cindy's name as author. Deep breath. Thump the keys. Suddenly, I was off. The title of my masterpiece in the making was *Back to Front*, in which mild-mannered secretary, Dervla Drizzle, was going to try anal sex for the first time at the hands of...

I received an email alert.

Fuck! What does she want?

I hadn't even written the book's blurb, the rough outline of where the story is headed with just enough information to whet the reader's appetite if not her pussy. I had no doubt most of my readers were women.

The 'she' in question was Sünsetia, my hard working and supremely talented German/Canadian designer whose covers were often the best things about my books. My words rarely lived up to the images she created. I suspect a lot of my sales were impulse buyers lured by the near naked hero and heroine in such lascivious poses that they got even my pussy puckering – and I don't actually have one. In my mind I become Cindy Ginger as I'm writing, right down to the anatomical variations. It is sometimes so real that I swear when I'm Cindy I suffer from PMT. At least Claudine says as much after I've sent off some of my rather curt emails about the promotion of my work or a particularly bad quarter of royalties.

"Honey, it's not my fault you ain't writing what the ladies want. Throw a bit of BDSM into the mix. A bit more Dom/sub. That's what the housewives with the boring husbands want. They want romance, danger.

They want to be swept off their feet by a handsome stranger who makes them capitulate."

That's all very well but Cindy has never been swept off her feet and dominated. The one and only time a man had attempted to tie me to the coffee table, he'd giggled so much it threw me off the scene. I informed him it wasn't working and he stormed off in a huff, leaving me bound and gagged until I managed to wriggle free three hours later, my skin rubbed raw where the rope had burned.

Sünsetia's email was flagged Urgent and Ignore This at Your Peril. I could, of course, pretend I wasn't home but as less than twenty minutes ago I'd sent her another of those beat-ups from the *New York Times* about a suburban housewife who'd uploaded as eBooks her twenty-five years' worth of bottom-drawer novels, rejected by every major and minor publisher in the business. As eBooks they'd been discovered by a readership so vast and so ravenous she'd become a millionaire practically overnight.

Some people have all the luck. And all the fuck.

I noticed Sünsetia had attached the cover jpg for *Alvin and the Chippendales*, Cindy's story about a country bumpkin, Alvin Hayseed, who comes to the city to make enough money to go back home to marry his voluptuous girlfriend, Titty Barnloft, but who gets in with a bad crowd and becomes a stripper with the Chippendales. Titty, as is the wont of all good heroines, misses her beau and goes chasing after him only to discover he's a bit of a bore really and she finds satisfaction in the arms of...

Damn, another email from Sünsetia.

I opened it carefully like it was a belt of plastic explosives ready to detonate at my slightest wince.

"Hi Cindy," it began as she always addresses me as the name on the book cover. I have so many pseudonyms sometimes even I forget who I am. "New directive just in from CashCow. They've banned navels and nipples on both male and females. Nothing we can do to appeal the decision which is a bit of a shame considering the cover has a whole chorus of male strippers naked to the waist sporting rather delectable navels. Easily fixed. I put cummerbunds around their waists. One problem solved. Bigger problem is their nipples. I can't exactly give them pasties. I tried and it looked ridiculous. I could give them the sorts of trousers our grandfathers used to wear, you know, the ones they used to hitch up under their armpits but it's definitely not sexy. Hmm, might appeal to all those grannies out there. So I've put vests on them. Have a look at the attached cover and give me your okay. This new morality is giving me a pain."

It's giving you a pain!

Sighing, I opened the jpg to be confronted by a monstrosity that was in no way Sünsetia's fault but what had once been a sizzling scene in a nightclub now looked like a row of waiters at a church social. What next, Titty in a burqua?

At least the bloody novel was out of the way and I only had to deal with the cover. *Sigh.* Back to the task at hand.

I typed in *Back to Front* in a type face I'd chosen specially for Cindy's work. Then my byline. Now, what was a good tag line to attract prospective buyers? Something succinct, to the point, sexy.

Dervla didn't know her ass from her elbow so Sir Simon Single, her handsome boss...

The phone rang. I'm sure the inhabitants of Alaska heard my cursing and I was still spewing forth expletives as I picked up the phone. I knew who it was. Claudine liked to take me by surprise, she used different phones every time she rang so her ID wouldn't come up on my phone. I'd learned, however, that she only had access to about a dozen different numbers and I'd programmed all of them into my phone. No way was I going to get taken by surprise.

As I was answering in words that contained no more than four letters and which began with S, C and F, I watched as my computer, which I'd programmed to catch any newly objectionable words in my stories, attacked my tag.

Dervla didn't know her ~~ass~~ [forbidden word] *from her elbow so Sir* [Is this appellation really necessary? It could be offensive to readers in the U.S. or else republican minded peoples outside the United Kingdom] *Simon Single, her handsome* [could be offensive to the beauty challenged] *boss* [Socialists might be turned off by the use of this word]...

Claudine was in one of her more frivolous moods. "My, my, we are testy today," she chuckled down the phone. I took a deep breath which warned her I was about to launch a broadside. "Now, now, don't get your knickers in a twist although I think after I tell you the latest directive from the CashCow bunker you'll probably want to wrap those knickers around your pretty little neck and hang yourself from the nearest rafter."

"What is it now, Claudine? I'm having the worst day imaginable. Bettany is demanding my new book, Sünsetia has just sent me the revisions for the cover of *Chippendales* and I have a toilet that's been blocked up all morning and I can't get a plumber to come out today."

She laughed down the phone which made me all the angrier. "You need your pipes unblocked? I would have thought you'd need more than a plumber to unlock yours. How long has it been? Years, I suspect. Don't call a plumber, you'll need an explosives expert to clear away the cobwebs in your pipes."

I tried to talk over her cackle but I'm not sure she heard me. "Very funny, Claudine, but you wouldn't be laughing if you had to shit in the shower and poke it down the drain hole with a stick."

She didn't hear me because she was still laughing and said merrily, "Hold on, honey. I think I've got just the man to fix the problem with your pipes." I heard her call her secretary before she muffled the mouthpiece. While she was busy I deleted backwards on my tag until all I had remaining was *Dervla didn't know...*

My thoughts were interrupted by the ping of a new email dropping in. I was on my business account at present so it was something I had to attend to. I groaned when I noticed it was from Bettany.

"Hi Tim, It's morning and there's no sign of your new story. I thought you said it would be here when I woke up."

I growled at the computer as if it were a living entity. "Not everyone gets out of bed at two in the morning, Bettany. Why can't you get up at a reasonable hour like everyone else?"

Of course, Bettany couldn't hear me; she was on the other side of the world. In the wilds of Scotland to be precise. Don't you just love how the internet has made the world so much more compact?

I was about to email back some snitty remark about civilized waking hours when I noticed the remainder of her email.

Fucking hell!

"The weather bureau has forecast a severe storm for the area, warning of gale-force winds, suggesting all houses in the area put up their shutters and ensure their power generators have sufficient fuel for at least a week. They're also forecasting some areas will be blanketed with snow. If the power lines go down, as they usually do in this sort of weather, then I'll be incommunicado for days if not weeks. I'm so far from the nearest town it sometimes takes the power people a fortnight to get here. So, in order to stick to your deadlines I need your latest opus by lunch-time today. My lunch-time, not yours. And I have my lunch around 10am. I'm looking forward to reading it."

She always signed off with love and kisses but currently I felt like strangling her with one of the Os or crucifying her on the X.

I tried to calculate the time in Scotland because they were so many hours behind us. I was jiggling numbers on my fingers wondering why the clocks weren't metric when everything else was when Claudine came back on the line, obviously very pleased with herself.

"One problem solved. The plumber will definitely be there today. I've used him before and he's very reliable. If he says he'll do something, he does it."

I breathed a sigh of relief. One less thing to take care of.

"On a more serious note. CashCow has decided it wants to pursue a policy of promoting family values but with an inclusive edge. So even though from now on any story containing sexual relations of any sort must only be between a married couple, and by that they mean married to each other, they will allow gay stories provided they're set in a state or country that currently provides for gay marriage. Good so far? So you'll have to get Alvin and Titty hitched before that romp in the barn. Okay? Simple enough for someone like you I would have thought. Bit of a problem later though when she falls for one of the Chippendale triplets but they each take turns having it off with her by deception. Not a chance, it seems. First, she'll have to divorce Alvin, and CashCow is not keen on divorce so you might have to kill him off which will leave her free to marry one, and only one, of the stripper triplets. More than one and it smacks a little too much of Mormonism. And none of this registry office nonsense either. It has to be the full church rigmarole. Anyway, I know you're a talented bastard so it should be no trouble at all to do a quick rewrite and whip it into shape."

My mouth was open to deliver a withering riposte but Claudine had already hung up.

I slammed my fingers down on the keyboard, deleting Cindy's title, name and first words. In a fury I typed *Pansy Prufrock and the Fairies Go Fishing* only to have it corrected seconds later with ~~*Pansy*~~ [offensive to gay men] *Prufrock and the* ~~*Fairies*~~ [see previous entry] *Go* ~~*Fishing*~~ [did you mean fisting? Fishing is a blood sport and not recommended for the entertainment of children].

"Oh, good lord," I shouted. If all the swearing in the world didn't do any good I suspect that appealing to a non-existent deity would fare little better.

I stormed out to the kitchen, shaking out a double dose of my blood pressure medication and washing it down with a tumbler of Scotch which, apart from making me decidedly wobbly in the knees, reminded me that time was ticking inexorably toward Bettany's lunch hour.

Back at the computer I sat in stunned stupidity trying to find the letters on a keyboard that wouldn't stay still. My fingers wouldn't take any notice of what my brain was telling them to do either. It didn't matter because suddenly my head slumped forward onto the desk and that's all I remembered until there was the sound of loud banging inside my head.

I started, wondering where the hell I was and why my head felt like it was full of clouds until I lifted it off the desk and suddenly it was full of throbbing pain. My mouth tasted of an old western bar-room with sawdust on the floor. The hammering began again and I realized it wasn't coming from inside my head. It was the front door.

Staggering to my feet, drool oozing from the corner of my mouth, one side of my face feeling like it had been flattened by the writing desk, I yelled, "Okay, I'm coming. Hold your horses."

It would only be someone trying to flog something because my friends knew better than to turn up unannounced. It seemed to take an eternity to find my way to the door but when I did I flung it open to show my annoyance at being interrupted in my work. "What?" I snapped.

Then I lost all reason. And my will to live.

He was six feet four of solid muscle. His biceps were the size of a baby's head, his chest was...well you could have served dinner on it. He had the most incredible washboard abs I'd ever seen... hang on! I realized I must have fallen asleep and tumbled into one of my own fantasy stories. I was dreaming, that was it.

How often does a semi-naked hunk, his torso shiny with perspiration and smeared with grease turn up at your door? Nah, couldn't be a fantasy. He was wearing shorts. If he were a fantasy, he'd be stark naked so I could see the cock that seemed to stretch the material in his tight shorts. Great legs. His feet were shod in work boots and that sexy turned-down socks look.

He smirked, obviously not offended by my ogling.

"Tim Marsden?" he enquired.

"That's me. I'll let you in on a little secret. The Tim is short for Timid."

I was shit-faced.

"Why Timid?"

"Cause I never have the courage to act on my impulses. Like now."

"What impulse would that be, Tim?"

"To lick all the sweat from your beautiful naked body."

"Might get grease all over your tongue if you tried that. Mind if I take a shower first?"

"First?" None of this made any sense.

"Then I'll fix your toilet. Claudine sent me."

Of course!

"Remind me to send her a thank-you note."

"Shower?"

"Uh? Oh, this way."

I led him to the bathroom and got him a fluffy towel. "You want a coffee or tea? Something to drink?'

"Coffee would be great."

"Okay." I leaned against the wash basin.

He coughed discreetly.

Definitely not a fantasy if he wanted me to leave.

"Nice wig, by the way," he said as he peeled off his shorts, revealing the most perfect hairless ass I'd ever seen. "Did you sleep in it?"

Shit! I slunk away to the kitchen and flinched when I glanced at myself in the mirror. I looked like a crumpled blanket, like someone had slept in me, and not in a good way. I'd totally forgotten I was dressed as Cindy Ginger to get my mind into character. I didn't go the whole cross-dressing route. Just a bit of lippy, eye shadow, tatty second-hand wig, a featureless smock and panty hose, but it was enough to get me in the mood. Okay, some people might think I went too far just to write dirty stories, but it worked. You should see me as Tex Steerhorn, my western pulp fiction pseudonym. Yee Haw!

I was such a loser. Forty-two years old and I was acting like a schoolboy. It's not like I hadn't been this close to God before. Yeah, as a matter of fact, I hadn't. I put the coffee on and stripped out of Cindy's gear and into Tim's. Tim would never have dared say what Cindy did at the front door even though he wanted it just as badly. I took two aspirin for my head and gorged on a number of dry crackers that I found at the back of the cupboard just to have something in my stomach.

By the time Mr. God emerged from the bathroom, the towel doubled over and wrapped around his waist I was pretty much sobered up.

"Coffee smells good," he said as he sat at my breakfast nook the shortness of the towel revealing just a little too much of his delectable balls. I didn't know where to look. I didn't think straight guys appreciated gay guys slobbering over their testicles. I observed his face. He was not a pretty boy type and he wasn't handsome. He was toward the rugged end of the scale and just this side of rough. You'd never call him good-looking in any way, in fact when he sneered, his face took on a sexually ugly allure. He gave off danger like most men give off testosterone.

God, he was gorgeous!

"Mm, that hit the spot," he said, putting his mug back on the table. "I had a quick look at your problem. Simple to fix. You just need a new ballcock. Lucky I have just what you need."

I spluttered my coffee everywhere, mopping it up with a tea towel. When I sat down, fidgeting nervously, he put his foot up on the spare seat so that I could look straight up under his towel. He was totally naked and his large cock lay like some sinister snake ready to strike. As I watched it began to move.

"Well, Timid Tim, you gonna help me out here or not?"

He loosened the towel from around his waist and it fell open revealing his whole magnificent body, his cock filling with blood and expanding to twice its original size. I didn't hesitate. I got down on my knees and shuffled over to him praying this was the kind of help he was asking for. If not, I'd risk dismemberment to get my mouth around that prick. I started with his balls, tonguing them, sucking them into my warm mouth. I was sorry he'd showered because I love the taste of a man's sweat.

"Oh, don't worry, Timid Tim, I saved some funky sweat for you," he said in the most dangerously seductive tones I'd ever heard.

"How—"

"I can read you like a book, Timid Tim. Like one of those trashy romance novels you write."

No one calls my books trashy and gets away with it.

"Shut your mouth, Timmy. Trash like you has nothing to say that I want to hear. You'll speak only when spoken to. Understand?"

I nodded my head. "Yes."

The slap stung my cheek. I hadn't seen it coming.

"Now let's try that again, shall we? You know the word you left out. One more thing, you'll speak only when spoken to, am I right?"

"Yes, sir," I said, lowering my eyes.

"No need for that, Timmy," he said lifting my face up by my chin. "I like it when cute older men worship me with their eyes. It's your way of acknowledging my superiority. I like that. You want to worship my body, Timmy?"

I was much more enthusiastic in my response this time. "Yes, sir."

"Good boy. As long as you obey every word, we'll get along just fine. Will you obey your master, like a good dog?"

"Yes, sir."

"Strip!"

I quickly removed all my clothes and piled them neatly on the kitchen table. I kneeled subserviently, awaiting instruction.

He stretched out on the chair, placing his arms behind his head so his biceps bulged almost as if the skin would split open and the muscle tear through. His hairy pits glistened.

"Right boy. Your master forgot to wash his pits. They need a good tongue bath. Hop up on my lap boy and get to work."

I straddled his thighs facing him, his cock pressing against my ass as I leaned forward to kiss his armpit. It was rank with perspiration and odor but I didn't care. It was so funky and muscular I could have died happy with my nose and mouth buried there. I licked the hairs, tasting his juice, swallowing it down. My cock was so hard I thought it would break. I licked every inch of his pit to clean it and then sucked the hairs and the skin until it was cleaner than had he scrubbed it in the shower.

I turned my attention to the neglected pit and repeated the process. I was in no hurry and he seemed happy that I took my time. When I'd completed my task he wrapped his powerful arms around me and pulled me to his chest encouraging my mouth over his nipple. It was hard so I sucked and nipped it lightly with my teeth.

"Bite it hard. Boy. It's not worth doing if it don't hurt."

I wasn't about to argue and I bit down hard enough for him to feel it. He sucked in his breath as the pain coursed through his body and I felt his cock twitch beneath my ass. I kneaded one bulging muscle, squeezing the pec tightly as I chowed down on the other, then swapped, and swapped back again. When he'd had enough he pushed my head down his body. I trailed my tongue across his grooved stomach as well as caressing the solid muscle with my hands.

What a magnificent specimen he was. Worthy of worship.

His cock poked insistently against my chest as my mouth moved lower down past his abs toward his neatly trimmed bush. I knew better than to wrap my lips around his cock until I was ordered to do so, so I contented myself with licking down between his thick thighs, getting my tongue into the crevasse between his groin and his legs.

I still couldn't believe my luck. Maybe I'd knocked myself out when my head hit the desk and this was all a dream. I knew it wasn't when he squeezed his legs together catching my head in a vise-like grip.

"I could burst your head like a fuckin' big pimple just by pushing my legs together. But I like you, boy. I like the way you make my body feel. I like the slutty way your tongue licks up my man sweat. Now, boy. Don't let me down. You just lay yourself down on the floor like a good dog. Yeah, that's it. Now I want you to clean my asshole. Make it shine. Get your tongue right up inside my shit hole. Understand?"

"Yes, sir."

He was squatting over my face, his ass crack opening so I could see his pink brown puckered raisin that I wanted to kiss so bad. My tongue slithered from my mouth eager to taste him. When he finally lowered his butt over my face I thought I would suffocate the fit was so snug. Because I trusted him, I began to lick his crack clean, swab away all the sweat and funk, swallowing it down like a gourmet cocktail.

He lifted off me and I took a deep breath.

"Good boy," he complimented before seating himself again. I began to tickle his sphincter with my tongue, easing it ever forward between the clenched muscle, withdrawing to bathe the anal entrance with my saliva or else sucking it, drawing it open. I pushed harder and bit by bit I managed to get my tongue farther into his canal. Periodically he lifted off to allow me to breathe. I hated that he had to do so as I didn't want to lose contact with that beautiful hole.

"You like that ass, boy?"

I mumbled my appreciation as best I could. It must have been the right answer because I received no punishment.

"Fuck, boy, you've sure got a tongue on you. Get it inside me, boy. Fuck my ass with your tongue."

He wriggled his butt over my face attempting to get more of me inside him. I rubbed my nose into his hole and pushed until he opened up. I inhaled deeply.

It was over too quickly and he sat back on the chair. He patted his knees. "Here, boy."

I sat back on his lap, eager for more. To my surprise he pulled my head back by yanking my hair painfully then planted his mouth over mine. He ran his tongue across my lips then pushed, forcing me to open up, his tongue exploring my mouth. I knew better than to push back unless requested to do so even though I had never been in this situation before.

"You're a natural, boy," he said taking time out from ravishing my lips.

It was uncanny the way he could almost read my thoughts.

His kiss made my insides melt. It was rough, demanding but full of warmth and such tenderness. I could fall for this big Neanderthal if I wasn't careful.

I sucked his tongue lightly in an effort to keep it buried in my mouth and he held my throat tight as he pushed his tongue until I thought he would reach my gullet. We broke apart to breathe, my heart beating like a drum.

"You're a sweet kisser, boy."

I dared a reply. "Thank you, sir. But not as good as you, sir."

He must have liked my reply because, again, there was no punishment.

"Up on the table on all fours like a good little doggy," he commanded and I was in position in next to no time.

"Do you trust me, boy?"

"Yes, sir."

"Good, then I want you to follow my instructions carefully and you'll be all right. I won't hurt you. Don't panic."

"Yes, sir."

"Now, just open your mouth. That's it. As wide as you can."

He poked the tip of his prick between my lips.

"No, don't try to suck my cock, boy. Just keep your mouth open."

I knew what he was going to do and I'm afraid I did panic a little. I'd seen it in straight porn movies and I marveled at the women who allowed men to fuck their face until phlegm and puke ran out their mouth and nose.

"Relax, boy. Relax, good doggy." He ran his hand through my hair until he felt my body get more comfortable. "Take a deep breath."

No sooner had I filled my lungs than he pushed his cock into my mouth so it plugged the back of my throat. He held my head in his strong hands while eight inches of thick solid prick ravaged my throat and my mouth. I hung on as best I could, feeling the sting of tears in my eyes, feeling the slime of puke and phlegm as strings of drool expanded and snapped as he withdrew only to ram back in again until I thought I could take no more. He fucked my mouth as if it were only a hole for his pleasure.

"Good boy, take a break while I get my tool kit."

Grabbing the tea towel I wiped the slime from my face, cleared my sore throat to make sure there was no permanent damage, and prepared for the next onslaught. I suppose I could have put an end to the torment but I had never been so turned on in my life. I had no wish to be anywhere else, to be anyone else. I wanted to be his sex slave.

Just as well because he returned with a length of cord.

"You still trust me boy?"

I didn't hesitate to say, "Yes, sir."

"Good, boy."

He roped me to the kitchen table.

"Not ideal, boy, but it will have to do."

It wasn't exactly uncomfortable but it wasn't comfortable either. I was on my back on the table my legs hoisted into the air bent at the knee, my arms roped to keep them in place. It meant my ass was vulnerable. He wasted no time in greasing my hole to slip an exploratory finger inside me having no difficulty locating my little pea of a prostate.

I bucked as he fingered it until my cock oozed precum.

Two fingers and then three until my ass opened up enough to take his cock.

It had been quite a while since Timid Tim had taken anything as big as this cock up his ass. Let's be honest here, it had been quite a while since Timid Tim had taken anything at all up his ass. Except in his fiction where he could take the most monstrous appendages known to man and erotica.

If my heroines could take eleven or twelve inches with nary a squeak of pain I'm man enough to take a mere eight. But real life isn't fiction and no amount of fantasy can compensate for the feel of real throbbing flesh and pulsating blood. As he plugged his hard gristle into my guts I almost swooned with the pain. Just like any good heroine would. But I wasn't a heroine. I was a horny slut who wanted cock.

I couldn't help myself.

"Fuck me, sir. Fuck my slut ass until I can't stand up. Make me your bitch, sir."

I waited for the abuse but instead Sir just pushed his cock into my willing ass until he was buried up to his balls. I gritted my teeth against the pain. Sir took his time so I could adjust to the pole invading my ass.

"Good, boy" he soothed. "I like my boys to beg."

Now that I had permission I was going to beg like the best of them.

"Fuck me hard, sir. Fuck my ass raw. Breed me. Pound my fuck hole until I bleed, sir."

"You are one for the filthy talk, aren't you, boy?"

"Yes, sir. Treat me like a filthy whore, sir. I worship you, I worship your body. You are my God, sir."

"Tell me about my body, boy."

"Your body is perfection, sir. Flex your muscles while you fuck my slut hole, sir. Let me worship you with my eyes while your big hard master cock tears my cunt to pieces."

He did flex his biceps as he pushed his cock in and out of my ass, but he preferred the more brutal grasp around my waist giving him better leverage to ram home all the harder.

"That's it, sir. Fuck your boy. Give it to me, sir. Shoot your spunk deep inside me."

I couldn't touch my cock and I wanted so much to come. I was on fire. He pounded me into the table pushing my body back against the cord that bound me. I couldn't move except to take my master's prick deep inside my bowels, screaming for him to use me, abuse me.

He hit my prostate again and again until, with a howl of pleasure, I shot my load onto my chest, opening my mouth to catch the stray bullet of spooge, swallowing it straight down. My sphincter gripped his pole, milking him as he plunged in and out finally making one last thrust and remaining still as I felt his cum shoot deep inside me.

He gave a few half-hearted thrusts to clear his balls of any late spunk, and then pulled out, wiping his greasy knob on my ass cheeks.

"Fuck, Man. Claudine told me you were inexperienced. If that's inexperienced, then I'm in the wrong business."

He wiped the perspiration from his forehead on a roll of paper towel and then soaked up the excess perspiration on my body, careful to leave the puddle of spunk on my chest.

"Claudine paid you to do this?"

"Yeah, man. She said you needed it."

"So, you're not a plumber?"

"Was. But I'm a cover model now for the sorts of shit you write."

"How come I've never seen you? I definitely would have noticed."

"Just starting out. Claudine said if I did this as a favor to her she'd make sure I got a series. She said there was more money in that."

"You going to untie me?"

"Sorry, mate. I gotta rush."

"Hey, you can't leave me like this."

He flipped open his mobile phone and dialed. "Hey, Kev, mate. Gotta job for you and any of the boys who like a bit of you know what on the side. Fuck, yeah. Great ass. You know me and ass, mate. Toilet, mate. Needs a new ballcock. And so does the owner. Needs as many new ballcocks as you can supply."

He winked at me.

"You'll have no trouble with him at all. I'm leaving him all wrapped up like a birthday present in the kitchen for you and the boys. Oh, he just loves plumbers, mate. Yeah, ciao."

He disconnected.

Slapping my ass, he smiled. "Thanks, boy. That was great. Maybe we can do it again some time."

"Anytime you're in the neighborhood," I said.

"You'll like Kev and the boys who are on their way over. They'll fix your problem and they'll show you a real good time. So you be the good little slut I know you can be and maybe they'll put you on their VIP program and they'll give your pipes a regular checkup. Would you like that, baby?"

"Yes, sir."

He chuckled as he let himself out.

Here I was trussed up on the table, my asshole itching for cock as Sir's cum leached out. How could I pass the time and stop myself from getting bored?

It was laughingly obvious. A new series. Of course. *U-Bend Over*, by Tim Marsden. It would need a very special model to bring out the sexy qualities of my plumber hero. Someone with the qualities of say, Sir.

I opened the keyboard in my mind and began to type.

CLIMBING UP THE WALL

The noises woke me. Loud voices and laughter. The irritating deep-throated opinions of a talk-back radio host. That's the problem with living in the inner city. Sounds. Everywhere. All the time. Personal silent space narrows considerably. No wonder so many people take up yoga. It's why I sleep in the back bedroom of the dilapidated inner-city terrace I rent. My bedroom backs on to a laneway – once a dunny lane for the easy collection and removal of euphemistically named 'night soil' – those thin wisps of public land recycled into herb gardens and pet basinets by the greedy, upwardly mobile who are moving into the area.

Mine simply ended up a repository for garbage and renovation detritus. Probably because all of us in the nine-house block are renters, not buyers, so we have no vampire-like hunger for a few extra square centimeters of backyard. I'm a night shift worker, so I sleep during the day. It's my problem because no one else knows or cares. That's what necessitated my move to the smaller bedroom. Away from the light. Away from the necessary decibels of everyday living on the street outside.

I blinked one eye open, peered at the clock until it came into focus, and groaned. I had been asleep for only ninety minutes. The sounds were unlikely to abate anytime soon. In fact, they were so close, they sounded as if they were coming from inside my head. I got out of bed to pad across the floor to close the window. It would be stuffy and humid, but I had to sleep. I scratched the itch in my balls. No one could see me as the bedroom window merely looks out on the painted back brick wall of the house opposite which blocks the sun until late afternoon. This enables me to leave the window open and the blind up and still kip in comparative gloom. It's particularly helpful in the sticky heat of summer.

My brain was as out of focus. Then it struck me. The voices were coming from above and below. People were in my backyard and on the roof. Burglars! I'd been broken into twice already in the short time I'd lived there, but this was the most brazen attempt ever. And they weren't being quiet about it.

As if to confirm my suspicions, the ladder propped over my window moved. What ladder? I didn't have a ladder. But someone did. And that someone was climbing up or down in preparation of breaking in via my very inviting open second floor window. I had to give them an "A" for audacity. Most thieves just jimmied the rotting woodwork on the ground floor window and scarpered in and out like larcenous cockroaches.

These guys were better organized. Probably more dangerous, too.

A boot appeared on the rung closest to the top of the window. The intruder was coming down. I could have run for the window and slammed it closed, but if these intruders were as brazen as they seemed, they'd have no hesitation in smashing the glass. I'd end up not only assaulted and battered, and bereft of personal electrical goods, but also left with a glazier's bill for a new window.

My hand closed round the handle of an ancient cricket bat that I occasionally used to prop up tables and beat to death inner city vermin. I waited. The boot became a naked leg emanating from a thick woolen sock curled over at the top, followed by tanned and almost hairless calves, then on to equally tanned thighs. My cock gave a twitch, which brought me back to the reality of my situation. I lifted the bat.

The cut-off jeans adhered to a bubble butt and a gift-wrapped full package of cock and balls like paint to a Picasso. The stomach muscles were firm, the belly button an innie and the pecs were…the pecs were…well, if I were the sporting type, I could have skied down them. I'm a chest man.

They say that when you are about to die your life slows and seconds seem like hours. That was happening to me now as I awaited my fate. The arms were strong and muscular as the body skittered further down the ladder. Strong enough to wrench my neck sideways, obliterating my life in an easy snap. The head…that same head I was about to batter into oblivion was…oh fuck! I couldn't tell whether the shallow breaths I was taking and the adrenaline beating of my heart was fear or lust. His eyes were blue. He was beefy, blond and beautiful. Not handsome. Beautiful, as you would describe an angel or some other ethereal being who was too good to be true. Like Billy in Jerry Mills' gay comic series "Poppers".

He was half-turned, calling to someone below, as I raised the bat. However, my dick was telling me that there were better ways of getting revenge. He stopped and turned fully. He blinked.

"What's the hold up?" his mate below yelled to him.

Blondie called down, "The guy's home after all."

"G'day, mate," he said to me in such a warm and friendly manner I almost forgot my intense dislike for the clichéd greeting. "Nice bat…and set of balls."

I realized I was totally naked, and erect, and that he was nodding in the direction of my tackle when he made the observation. I dropped the cricket bat and grabbed for my briefs that were on the end of the bed. I had trouble pulling them over my erection, and it poked over the top of the elastic waistband even more obscene than my original nakedness.

"Don't you just hate piss pricks?" he said.

His mate continued to call impatiently from below.

"Hold your horses. He wants to discuss indoor cricket."

There was a snort of derision from the backyard.

"Sorry to disturb you, mate," he said. "Hard night?"

I explained that I was a night worker and...what the hell was I doing discussing my sleep patterns with a fucking burglar?

"Didn't you get the landlord's note?" he asked with a comical arch of an eyebrow.

"The...?" Then it hit me. A month ago a note had been slipped under my door telling me the landlord was finally going to fix the problem roof and guttering that leaked like a sieve every time it rained, smearing a moldy stain across a corner of the bedroom ceiling.

"Oh shit." I wasn't going to die after all. The split second thought of the relationship between danger and my erectile performance I filed for analysis at another time. Interesting. But later.

"You wanna come in?" I asked meekly.

"I don't think there's enough room in there for you, me and that!" he said nodding in the direction of my blood engorged cock.

I grinned. "I'll open the back door."

He okayed the idea, scrambling down as agilely as...well, a cat burglar.

A few minutes later, I had the coffee on. It was the least I could do as a peace offering. They dumped their tools near the door, asking if they could store them in the house to save bringing them back every day. I didn't dare ask how long they'd be on the job in case I gave away my enthusiasm for a slow completion date.

Stig introduced himself with a handclasp that sent sparks of longing through my whole body. He had been raised in Australia by his mum, but his dad was Swedish.

His surly mate was Egon, a darkly attractive German, who grunted rather than phrased recognizable answers to any of my questions. They told me of the upheaval my life was to undergo in the next few weeks right down to my having to move to the front bedroom while they cut out part of the ceiling, re-plastered it and replaced recalcitrant bricks under the eaves of the roof. Surprisingly, I was overjoyed at the news.

They finished their coffees, and I told them I'd leave the back door open so they could use the kitchen and bathroom any time they wanted.

"Most people don't even like us to come inside the house," Egon whined.

"Yeah, mate, that's mighty good of you," Stig enthused. "We'll do a bang up job for you; get outta your hair real quick."

"Oh, no need to hurry," I stammered.

"Back to work," Egon told his work-mate, depositing his empty coffee mug in the sink.

Stig grabbed a handful of crotch through his shorts and muttered playfully, "Eat me, cocksucker!" Then he looked at me quickly and muttered, "Sorry, mate."

"That's okay, just builders talk, I know." I could forgive this guy just about anything.

I don't know if it was deliberate, but Stig bent over to pick up his tool belt and his tank top rode up so I could catch a glimpse of that exquisite sweaty butt crack topped with a fuzz of blond foliage. I got hard instantly. Egon noticed me staring. He didn't look impressed. Jealous, perhaps?

Telling them to call me before they left so I could lock away their gear, I went, reluctantly, back to bed. This time, though, I closed the window and pulled the curtain, leaving just enough so that I could watch glimpses of Stig as he shimmied up and down the ladder. They kept their noise to a minimum, but I still couldn't sleep. I kept watching the chink in the curtain hoping for another glimpse of Stig's plastic-perfect skin, mixed by the most exquisite palette and sprayed on with an artist's airbrush. No amount of instructing my body to sleep was going to get it to obey with that in the vicinity.

I pulled down the sheet and began to massage my cock, which was already half hard. It was demanding attention and would not let me have any peace until I helped it out. I stroked it as I thought of Stig and his luscious mouth closing round my knob, his tongue flicking at the slit…I slowly bent the naked builder over the edge of my bed and pulled his ass crack apart, aiming my hard-on at the moist, inviting hole. I plunged, he grunted…But every fantasy conjured up in my mind had Egon in the background. Watching. Glaring possessively.

The following week was agony. Stig's presence was enough to send me dizzy with thwarted possibilities. Egon did thaw a little, showing me photos of his wife, and daughter, Louisa. They made a beautiful family. He was a little older than Stig, perhaps 30 or so, with a moss of dark hair on his chest. He was less beefy, less gregarious, but I noticed a definite change in the tone of his grunts. Stig, it seemed, had no photos of family or even girlfriends, as they came and went as frequently as he came and went. Or so Egon would have me believe. Stig merely confirmed the stories with a blush that looked like it had been applied by a celestial make-up artist.

The beginning of the second week, Stig arrived on his own. I usually waited up for them with a pot of freshly brewed coffee. They liked that and sat and nattered for about 15 minutes before starting work. I would then head off to bed and my attempt at a Stig-induced wet dream.

"Where's Egon?" I asked, hoping this would be my opportunity.

"Louisa is sick. He had to take her to the doctor," he said as he slurped his coffee with cream and two sugars. I'd bought doughnuts on my way home from work that morning and told him to help himself.

"Ta, mate," he said as he took one and dunked it in his coffee.

"That's very American," I commented as he put it to his mouth.

"What is?" he said.

"Dunking doughnuts."

"It's okay, isn't it?" he asked with some slight concern lest he be breaking some gastronomic rule about doughnuts.

I laughed. "Of course it is. You just don't see many Aussies doing it." He looked a bit bewildered and went to dunk again, but hesitated. "Go on," I said.

He laughed and did as he was told. Oh, that he would do everything that easily.

"His daughter okay?" I asked.

"Just a virus, he thinks. He'll be here soon."

Stig finished up and took the ladder out into the backyard.

"You need a hand?" I yelled.

"Nah, mate. She'll be right,"

I made my way upstairs and got into bed. If Stig was around much longer, I was definitely going to become sexually dysfunctional. I would have to encourage them to finish up as soon as they could. That way, Stig would be gone and I'd get my life back.

Suddenly, there was a thundering crash and a loud shout. I bolted out of bed and down the stairs. I wasn't naked this time as I'd learned to wear my briefs to bed while the builders were around.

I laughed out loud. The extension ladder had come apart, and Stig had fallen on to my favorite ornamental chili plant, which was now beyond salvation. He looked so hurt and embarrassed, sheepishly wiping the back of his shorts clean of soil; I couldn't have bawled him out.

"You okay?"

"Sure," he said. "Just a little spill." But when he attempted to get the ladder, he hobbled and almost fell.

I rushed to help him. This was the first time I had touched that skin. It was smooth as icing on a cake.

"Maybe I had better sit down for a minute," he mumbled. He'd been badly shaken and looked quite pale.

I helped him inside and before he sat down, I noticed specks of blood on his shorts.

"I think you may have cut yourself. You're bleeding."

"Where?"

"Your butt."

He tried to turn his head, but grimaced in pain.

"Let me have a look," I offered. "Here, bend over the end of the couch. As he did, I slid his shorts down a little. Yes, those melon-like cheeks had scraped and very small spots of blood dotted his rump. And some of the hardier twigs of the chili bush had protested their demise by jabbing into his flesh.

"Um, I may have to pull your shorts down further." It took a lot to keep my voice under control.

"It hurts like hell back there."

His shorts came off, and I whistled at the beginnings of a purple bruise. I touched it gently. "That hurt?"

He winced. "Hurts like fuck."

I tried to cheer him up. "Want me to kiss it and make it better?"

"If you think it will help," he guffawed.

It was now or never.

I leaned over and pressed my lips to the bruise.

"Better?" I said.

"A little to the left."

I moved toward his ass crack and kissed again.

"Nice," he whispered. "But maybe over a little more."

I didn't hesitate. I gently prized apart his ass cheeks, putting my lips to his fragrant hole.

He moaned. "Yes, right there."

I licked gently at his blond, tanned ass. This boy obviously went to nude beaches because the tan went all the way. I maneuvered my tongue into his hole, lapping at the doorway to his guts. I wanted to lube him good before I pounced. Nothing was going to stop me from planting my cock inside him. I spat into his inviting hole, then on my cock before I stood up and leaned over him.

"Will this make you feel better?" I asked.

"Better than better," he croaked through a mixture of desire and pain.

He grunted as my cock pushed aside the flesh of his sphincter, whether from pain or pleasure I wasn't sure. I tried to avoid contact with the bruise on his ass, which meant I could not push in my full length. .

"Slam it right in to your balls," he demanded.

"I don't want to hurt you."

"Fuck that. This is the best hurt I've ever had. It was worth every bit of pain."

I pushed gently into him until his warm sock of an asshole slid smoothly around my cock.

"What do you mean?" I picked up the pace.

"You know how hard it is to throw yourself off a ladder when you're as safety conscious as me?"

He turned his head as best he could to look at my reaction. "How else was I gonna get you to look at my ass?"

"I look at your ass every single day you're here," I said. "I can't take my fucking eyes off it. All you had to do was ask."

He grunted his appreciation with every thrust. "I don't know how to," he said. "It's easier with girls."

I pulled out.

"Hey, don't stop," he pleaded.

I led him upstairs to the bedroom. I wanted to watch this beautiful creature while I fucked him. I lay him on his back and told him to hold his legs back behind his head, exposing his beautiful, pink, swollen tunnel. I knelt down and kissed it again. Then I kneeled over him, pushing until he swallowed me right up to my balls. I wanted to push them inside him, too. I leaned forward as I prized open his lips with my tongue. I met a brief resistance. I licked his lips and sucked gently on his tongue. He returned the favor, our mouths opening wide as if attempting to suck out each other's brains. When we came up for air, he wiped his mouth with a quiet, "Wow." He knew guys fucked one another, but he didn't know they kissed, he told me later.

I stroked his thick, blond cock as I picked up pace. He arched his ass toward me, moving to meet my strokes, squeezing his sphincter muscles around me, trying to absorb me totally. I gasped as his ass spasmed and he shot a load all over his chest. I pulled out, co-mingling my cum with his, howling as my squirts hit his chest. I collapsed and made swirling cum paintings on his stomach with my fingers.

Now comes the awkward part, I thought to myself. But Stig wasn't finished. He ignored his discomfort and leaned down to put his mouth over my cock.

"I want to taste you," he said shyly.

I flinched as those wet lips closed around my rod.

"What's wrong?" he asked. "Am I doing it wrong?"

I laughed, moving my body so my mouth was over his still leaking prick – and engulfed it.

His whole body bucked. "Holy fuck!" he shouted.

Then we heard movement downstairs.

I threw on some clothes, gave Stig a towel because his shorts were still in the living room, and as nonchalantly as we could we went downstairs, Stig leaning heavily on me for effect rather than necessity.

"What's going on?" Egon looked up.

"I fell off the ladder," Stig said simply.

"Was the ladder in the bedroom?" he asked sarcastically.

Stig lied. "I had to lie down. I was in so much pain."

"Can you work today?" Egon asked, although his concern sounded remarkably like sarcasm.

"Yeah, I'm just bruised." Stig turned to show him.

Egon picked up his shorts and threw them to him. "Put your clothes back on." When he stood up, I noticed the outline of a not unsubstantial weapon in Egon's pants, plus a tell-tale spreading stain. He had either seen or heard what was going on, or he had one helluva vivid imagination.

Stig noticed, too. "I think I might stay like this a little longer."

Egon looked miffed. "As you please."

"No need to act like you got the rags on," Stig retorted. "There's plenty for you if you got the guts to take it." With that, he grabbed Egon's crotch and squeezed. Egon pushed his hand away like he'd been burned. "That's up to you, mate." He shrugged, patting his ass. "But it can be yours any time."

I twinged with jealousy. Stig would never be mine for more than a quick grope but, still, on our wedding day I had expected some sort of commitment.

"It could have been you, mate," Stig continued to Egon. "Except you've always been too scared. Those crap photos of your wife and daughter. Don't you think I found out long ago she's your sister and her kid. Why pretend, mate? You slobber over me behind my back. You can fire me if you want 'cause it's your builders license, but I'm gonna tell you something first. From now on, every morning when I come to this job, I'm gonna have me some fun before we start. I'm gonna do it on my own time, but I'm gonna do it every day. Or, at least as often as he wants it." He pointed to me sheepishly.

"Every day," I managed to croak.

"And if he'll let you, you can join in. You don't mind if he joins in do you, mate?" Stig asked.

He was so polite about it I could scarcely refuse.

The stain on Egon's work trousers was spreading. But he made no answer. After a long pause, Stig grabbed his own shorts and gingerly pulled them up over his butt. He gave my lips a long tongue-lashing and winked before he headed outside. He slapped me on the ass and told me to get some sleep.

Over the next few days and weeks, as the job slowly crept to completion, Stig blossomed under our morning fuck sessions. It was the third day before Egon appeared at the door to watch, and another before he hauled out his rock solid cock to jerk off as he watched Stig buried to his balls in my ass. Two days later, he tentatively put his cock in Stig's mouth. His education proceeded at a slower pace, but he was learning.

Stig bought me a bigger and better chili plant. Then one day, the job was complete. Egon fucked Stig that day. It was the first time.

I was buried up to my balls in Stig's tight, blond butthole, realizing this was my last opportunity to pork his incredible Viking body good and hard. Egon, as usual, was stuffing his mouth with the subtlety of a steroidal Romanian weightlifter, choking him until his lips and face were slimy with gag puke. That's the way the German seemed to like it. Stig was happy to oblige his buddy. Sinking my prick deep into his butt, his ass muscles flexed, attempting to hold me inside, but I pulled out to watch my shank sink its entire length slowly back between those wrinkled lips. That gaping hole felt so good. It excited me to watch my throbbing cock disappear into the clenching, insatiable body. I picked up speed, fucking Stig hard enough that I was pushing him forward, impaling his mouth on Egon's rampant cock. The sight of that cute face taking dick all the way down his throat was almost enough to make me blow, but I slowed again, wanting the moment to last.

But between the glorious vision of Stig's pouting mouth bludgeoned by big, buff German sausage and his pulsating asshole squeezing the juice out of my balls, I lost control, machine gunning my load into his guts. I grunted in ecstasy and in despair. It was all over.

To my surprise, Egon pulled his saliva slick stub from Stig's mouth, flipped his young blond companion on to his back, and was kneeling against Stig's slimy asshole, pushing hard, before either of us knew what had happened. Stig let out a bellow of surprise as Egon breached his ass gate and sank his full length is split seconds. Once the pain had subsided and the surprise had worn off, Stig relaxed into the embrace of the man he had been encouraging for weeks. The German leaned in to kiss him, while caressing his silky hair, whispering just before their lips met, "You belong to me now."

As I watched, I saw how well suited to each other these two were. The dark complimenting the light. I felt like an intruder.

Stig pulled me to him for a kiss. "Don't be sad," he said. "It was the only way I could think of to get him."

I left the room quietly, leaving them to it.

The day after, they packed away their tools, of both persuasions, and headed off for their next job. I went out to a hardware store and bought a ladder. I propped it against the window. It was there for two weeks. Then I reluctantly took it away.

LITTLE RED RIDES DA HOOD

The mayor was much more solicitous than I had any right to expect, until I looked at him closely, his piggy jowls, his sweating forehead, and flashed back to a press conference a few years prior where he told the world, "Graffiti is an urban blight. It is no more 'art' than the rubbish scribbled on the walls of public lavatories. Graffiti, whatever its claims to 'street art,' is vandalism. Pure and simple."

He'd certainly changed his tune.

"We managed to save many of your works, moving them to more stable environments, areas where they will be better appreciated," he turned his attention to me.

What he meant was more upscale suburbs, not the public housing estates where I grew up and created the work. He pointed out one of my early tags emblazoned on a slab of marble at the entrance to the new cultural center. I would have been impressed if I'd been into that sort of public approbation. I wasn't. Either impressed or into that sort of acceptance. I was even less impressed that the work in question was not mine. It was a very good facsimile, I'll grant the artist that, but it had been copied from a photograph or from memory. It had none of my sweep. The colors were wrong, less vibrant than I would use. The curvature did not have the lines of a supple erect male penis which is the model upon which I based it.

"Stop the car," I called to the driver.

"We're late already," the mayor complained.

"Stop the car now!" I wasn't going to argue with some petty bureaucrat who was obviously using me to attract votes from people who were not normally his natural constituents.

With a sigh that signaled he was complying under duress, the mayor instructed the driver to pull over near the monument. I scrambled out of the vehicle. The welcoming party of officials, arty types and brown nosers could wait. Running my fingers across the granite I remembered where I had first sprayed a symbol like this, and it hadn't been across a piece of stone. It was on the side of a brick shithouse near the tower block in which my step brother and me were trying to make ends meet. Mostly unsuccessfully.

"It was valued at quarter of a million dollars by Sotheby's," the mayor shouted above the din of the passing traffic.

Obviously some wanker who had no idea of art. Anyone who knew anything at all about my work knew

I'd never sprayed on granite. Nothing so grand. It was always brick, fibro, brick veneer, aluminum, and glass, anything that the neighborhood harbored in abundance. Corrugated iron was the thing. It was used to board up the windows and doors of deserted housing on the estate. It had been used to board up our place after me mum died. Never knew me dad. Nor did Biff, me elder brother. Half brother. Same mum, different dads. Mum never kept a man around long enough for either one of us to bond with 'em.

I still find meself slipping into the old ways. Especially in me thinking. Dropping 'g's, saying 'fink' instead of 'think', 'me' instead of 'my', the sorts of fings that label you as common. Or vulgar.

You know what? I miss it. For all the fame and the bullshit that surrounds me now, for all the grand art galleries and museums around the world that clamor for me work, I was happiest here, when I worked on the streets, frightened I'd be picked up by the cops, scared I'd be picked on by one of the gangs that staked out their territory like dogs pissing against lamp posts, defending it to the death. I was part of all that ten years ago, and yet not part of it.

I opened the bag I carried with me wherever I went and was shaking the spray can before the mayor could even disengage his seatbelt to open the limo door. I heard him scream for me to stop, that I was defacing a work of art, supposedly my work of art mind you. When I'd made my little additions, I ran across the roadway, car horns blaring at me like nagging adults, and then disappeared down a side street, leaving the mayor gaping at my simple message: *This is bullshit!*

That should add another hundred thousand to the value of the piece. I'd even signed it with my tag. I'd get my agent onto it later to have it declared a site of national artistic importance before they could wash it off or paint it over. That would be one in the eye for the establishment.

Okay, so I knew it was a juvenile tilt at windmills but, God, did it feel good. Not only to give those arty-farty types the finger but also to be back where it all began. I was on a high as I escaped my escort and careened past the so-called cultural center, amazed at the sprucing up the old neighborhood had undergone; until I reached the car park. It was all a facade. Like a Hollywood streetscape, a frontage, frosting to disguise the rot behind.

There was a forlorn park out back of the center, on the other side of the entrance to the underground car park. Rusting children's slippery dips and swings were barely hidden by a line of trees obviously meant to shield concertgoers from the horrors that lay beyond. The horrors of poverty and deprivation, lives swept under the carpet. Nothing obvious from the main road.

It shouldn't have thrilled me, but it did. Scratch the surface and the suppurating sore was revealed. This was 'home.' This was where I thrived. This was where I got me inspiration, something that was in very short supply of late. This was where I became 'me.' There was another reason for the excitement that coursed through my body.

I couldn't see it yet, but I knew it had to be here. I was thrown off slightly by the cultural edifice behind me, struggling to get my bearings. I spun around and around until I spotted it, squat and ugly as it had always been. I ran toward it like an old friend.

It was the squalid toilet block where my real life began. Where I first began my graffiti. Where I first discovered my predilection for men. Walking around it, I admired its ability to endure; running my fingers across the battered brickwork where once my art had adorned the outside walls until an embarrassed city council had steam cleaned away my painted frustration at the futility of my life, although leaving remnants of color still staining the cement.

I was surprised to find it open. It was ten years since I'd been here and still it smelled of piss and stale farts, booze and baby batter. Without worrying about the consequences, I stepped inside. It was dingy, the plumbing ripped from the walls, the urinal caked with rust and piss stains. Surprisingly, the three cubicles still had their doors intact to shield the modesty of the occupants. My work had been all but obliterated by countless graffiti artisans since my basic scrawls. And, of course, the ubiquitous invitations to partake of sexual pleasures on such and such a date, long since passed, or the open invitation to be here on a Tuesday at 2pm for the 'blow job of your life.'

Opening my backpack I found my spray cans and began to transform the first cubicle. You could probably accuse me of ego but the senseless scribbling and territorial markings revealed an appalling lack of ambition. I tied a bandana across my nose before I shook the can, that metallic marble rattle sending sparks to my dick. I was always hard when I made my art, probably due to a combination of the frightening prospect of being caught and the fact I was indulging in the graffiti artist equivalent of flashing.

It took a scant ten minutes before I'd turned the first cubicle into a cock-tinged bordello. If any man could sit on the stainless steel lav – they were new – and not get hard then he was either blind or dead. I was about to move on to the second when I heard the tell-tale scrape of shoes on the gravel outside. That was the usual early warning system queers gave one another on approach. My heart was racing. It might just be the police looking for a quick arrest, a gang on the prowl for a poofter to bash, or, I checked the date on my watch, Mr. Blow Job of Your Life. I didn't even consider the possibility it was someone with a legitimate excuse to use the public convenience.

I could have walked out and explored my other early haunts but that tingle you get in your crotch when you're up for adventure was keeping me rooted to the spot. I bolted the door and sat on the rim of the bowl, my cock drooling in anticipation, the adrenalin pumping through my system. I unzipped to give my anxious prick room to move, keeping it in line of sight of the glory hole cut so perfectly through the wall separating each cubicle.

Someone cleared his throat, another early warning, scraped his feet, and then pushed lightly at my door even though it would have been showing Engaged on his side. He then pushed the door of the cubicle next to mine and entered, shuffling to bolt the door behind him. Tearing off sheets of cheap toilet paper, he wiped down the rim before lowering his jeans and briefs to perch on the bowl. I know because I was watching him through the glory hole.

I dared not lean in close enough to see his face. It was irrelevant anyway. Cute or handsome was an extra but totally unnecessary. Here, it was the cock that counted. Frustratingly, I couldn't see his as the T-shirt hung low and covered his crotch. I coughed, wondering whether he was Mr. Blow Job or whether he was here to be blown. Either way, I could accommodate. When I peeked again, he had lifted his offending top to reveal a slim, long prick with hairy balls. I'd say just the way I like them except I like cocks in all shapes sizes and colors of the rainbow.

He was slowly milking his prick and I wanted a taste. I kneeled on the filthy floor, pushing my index finger through the hole beckoning him to feed me. I heard him shuffle then his dick breached the wall between us. I didn't have to be asked twice and wrapped my lips around the circumcised head and ran my mouth down the shaft to give him a taste of paradise, just like I did all those years ago when I spent as many of my waking hours here as I could.

There weren't too many places I could go at eighteen. My only friends were my spray cans, I'd carried them and their brothers since I was fourteen, using them as a weapon against my loneliness, scrawling my anger on walls until I learned to channel my energies into art, shit I hate that word, and later into sex.

They say "there's no place like home." Not where I lived. Rundown smack house where mum had OD'd and dad...well, I had no idea who dad was except he was one of the many uncles who dropped in to see mum when she needed money for a fix. My stepbrother brought me up. I suppose that's too strong a term for the fact he allowed me the use of a bedroom as long as I kept out of the way when he did his deals or he had his gang members over.

When I was younger I looked up to him, admired him, and wanted to be him. He'd grab me in a headlock and ruffle my hair until I struggled, laughing all the while. He was six years older than me and, as I hit puberty, I became a nuisance. I didn't grow much; I was always little at five foot six. I could still wear the clothes mum had bought when I was fourteen. Just as well because she never bought me another stitch. I would have run the streets naked if it hadn't been for my skills at shoplifting.

That was the age I was when I saw the most dazzling thing I ever set eyes on. A crimson hoodie. It knocked the wind out of me. I literally gasped when I saw it. It was the most beautiful thing I'd ever seen. Hey, I was fourteen, cut me some slack. I had to have it. Every afternoon, after school, I would turn up at the department store and practically drool over this piece of clothing. If it had had a hole I probably woulda fucked it.

There was no way I was ever gonna steal the fucker. Security knew me by sight and kept a close eye on me. So did the CCTV cameras in the store. Nah, the only way I could get this hoodie was to pay for it. I trembled when

I sought out the price sticker and my heart sank when I discovered it was $59.99. No way was Biff gonna give me the money. Maybe he'd pay me to run some of those errands I did for him when he was busy. He laughed at me for my trouble.

I look back on me at that age and can't believe the determination I had. I ended up getting a job stacking shelves in a 24-hour convenience store for this Arab guy called Ahmed. He liked the way I stacked the shelves real neat and tidy. He also liked the way my asshole gripped his dick as he pounded me in the back room when business was slow. He was the one who told me "You were born to be fucked, boy. In the mouth. In the ass." It was the first compliment I ever received. Well, I took it as a compliment.

But I soon learned the true meaning of capitalism. I got lousy wages for shelf stacking and for bending over and taking the boss's prick on a regular basis, I got a peanut bar or a chocolate. Even at my age that didn't seem like a fair exchange. Even less so when Ahmed began to introduce a few of his mates to me. Most of them married, with kids, some even the same age as me.

It wasn't as if these guys were the first but they sure taught me things I hadn't known before. I had to thank them for their refining my technique but, more importantly, they taught me the value of blackmail. Suddenly I had my coveted red hoodie, paid for in cash, plus a bit of spare pocket money. Biff thought I'd stolen it but when he discovered I'd paid ready money, he became suspicious. I told him I was blackmailing some old geezer whose secret I'd overheard in the shop. That made him dead proud and he resorted to the headlock of old.

I drank in his odor and his warmth while he held me. I got hard. Biff kept himself in good nick, and didn't he know it. He swaggered everywhere, never walked. Always had his shirt open to show his chest, his abs and just enough of his underpants to turn on the sluts that hung round him like seagulls round a fishing port. I knew why they flocked to him. I'd seen it. Accidentally. His cock. A living treasure. Long, thick and creamy. I'd seen it in action. He never tried to hide it when he had his bitches over. He never closed his bedroom door and if I got up in the night to go to the bathroom he didn't mind me standing getting an eyeful.

He did them every which way, shooting his cum in their twats, or down their throats or, my favorite because I could see all his lovely spunk, over their faces. I'd rush back to my bedroom and fantasize it was my face as I whacked off, shooting a load into my sticky sheets.

The only downside to Biff's admiration for my entrepreneurial skills was his hatred for my hoodie. Hatred is too mild a word. He loathed and detested it. That was where I learned strength, or to give it a more correct term, stubbornness. The more Biff ridiculed me, the more I dug in my heels until I loved the bloody thing more than life itself. It became a symbol of my independence.

Biff wouldn't let me join his gang – fine! There were other outlets I'd find. He called me names – Little Red was his favorite putdown – so to defy him I'd only answer to the name Red from then on. We were both so pissed off at each other we drifted apart. Fuck him! It wasn't like he was a great source of support or affection. I'd find encouragement elsewhere. I knew just the place.

I found loads of affection. And those loads usually ended up in my ass or my stomach, sometimes on my chest or in my hair or over my face. It was messy but it showed me I was loved.

Here I was sucking cock again in the same shithouse. Thirty fuckin' years old and still searching for love on the end of a dick. Would I never learn? Well, no, not while the cocks were as juicy as the one I had in my mouth at that moment. All too soon, my unseen partner gasped and shoved his cock hard through the partition. I kept my mouth suctioned to his prick as I gulped down his warm sperm, my nose crushed against the wall.

He pulled out and zipped up, disappearing without so much as a thank you. I laughed to myself. It was such a solitary pursuit, either side of the cubicle wall, just one step up from jerking off.

I didn't have much time to think about it because I was still on my knees day dreaming when another guy took his place on the stainless steel bowl. He was much less modest than his predecessor and had his jeans down round his ankles, he wore no underwear, and hoiked his shirt up over the hairy belly that almost covered his cock. When he leaned back against the wall though his short, stubby prick reared its reddish angry head.

I beckoned again with my finger, rewarded with a weapon that stretched my lips almost to breaking point. I was afraid my teeth would scrape the delicate skin of his shaft, wishing I could dislocate my jaw. Fortunately, I could control the pace and my lover had to be content with whatever I was prepared to give.

He must have liked it because he whispered just loudly enough that I could hear, "Shit, boy, you've got a mouth on you. I could fuck that throat of yours all night."

Then it hit me. Of course, I was never going to get my cock sucked by Mr. Blow Job. The message was one I'd written a decade ago, a message that had men lining up to use my mouth, my body for a few moments of happiness. It alone had remained of all the graffiti, men obviously hopeful of my return one day. That was a monument worth having.

"I could fuck that throat of yours all night," he repeated.

I shuddered because it was words similar to those that ten years ago started the inevitable tragedy that followed. Tragedy depends on the way you look at it, I suppose. It led to my success in the long run, although the immediate consequences were devastating.

I'd been down on my knees, slobbering over a particularly nice piece of meat, my throat raw from all the poking it had endured as well as the sea of spunk that I'd swallowed that afternoon, when the john I was servicing whispered, "Your mouth is like a fine cunt, boy. Milk me with your lips, fag boy."

I'd been called all sorts of names while kneeling in this position, and this was an affectionate use of the term, not like when fag bashers spat it out like venom. Yeah, dirty words turned me on and, if I was truly honest with myself, the idea that I was in a filthy crapper down on my hands and knees sucking the juice out of anonymous cocks made my own dick hard as hell. I usually shot my load two or three times in an afternoon. Sometimes one of the guys would ask to reciprocate and I'd always let him, but it was rare. Mostly my mouth was the cum dump.

This guy kept it up, complimenting me on my skill, telling me I was better than his girlfriend. I wasn't stupid enough to believe him. Guys will say anything to get blown. I made it a rule never to peek through the hole above the waist to see what the guy looked like. I loved the anonymity of it, besides I didn't know how I would react if it was someone I knew.

Yeah, I had regulars who knew where to find a good time with no strings attached. Just dump'n'go. I was always careful never to wear my red hoodie on the days I siphoned spunk, I was too well known in the 'hood. The anonymity thing worked both ways. Fags didn't have a long life expectancy on the estate.

I was stupid. I admit it. But after years of getting my throat fucked or pushing my ass up against the wall I wondered what it would feel like for real human contact. Shit, I was nineteen and never been kissed, not surprising considering that after an afternoon on my knees my breath must have smelt like a sperm bank.

I was vulnerable. When the guy started whispering that he wanted to ram his dick up my ass without the impediment of the wall, to slap his balls against my butt, to hold me around the waist, well, I was a sucker, no more, no less. I should have got out of there straight away.

"Come on, boy, you know you want to feel me skin to skin. I can sink it deeper inside your insatiable little hole, make you feel like a good little slut. Treat your fag cunt the way it should be treated."

He did have a nice juicy piece of meat that would feel real good wedged in my butt right down to the balls. But no amount of desire could overcome my sense of self preservation. If my secret ever got out I would be dead meat. I refused in as few words as I could muster and made it as friendly as possible. But he kept begging and bellowing as I attempted vainly to drain his balls so he'd quit his bellyaching.

But the more effort I put into it the more he wanted my ass. I stood, backing onto his massive prick. That quieted him for a moment, but he started up with his skin-on-skin routine. I clenched my ass muscles around his prick but that just encouraged him to demand more. I calculated the risk of pulling off his cock and making a run for it.

It's almost as if he anticipated my thoughts because he pulled out, then I heard the door of his cubicle slam open. The only protection I had was the door to mine which was firmly bolted. The builders had obviously reckoned without the strength of the horny guy who was banging on the flimsy door as the bolt gave way easily, the door to my cubicle swinging open.

I froze. The smile disappeared off the face of the massive guy standing in the doorway, his prick leaking onto the concrete floor, as I attempted to hoist up my jeans. I could almost hear the cogs grinding as he thought through his situation. Then he beamed.

"Well, fuck me!" he chuckled.

I knew I was in deep shit.

He ambled into the cubicle, slamming the door closed, stroking my face as he drew it toward his prick.

"Does Biff know what his baby bro gets up to during the day?" he asked malevolently. I didn't have to shake my head, because he went on without pause. "No, I bet he doesn't. What do you think he'll say when he finds out?"

I looked him in the eye. "About the same as what your gang will think of you when they find out."

He grabbed me by the throat, squeezing hard. "But they won't find out about me. Anyone rats and they're dead." He let me go. "Besides, it ain't me down on my knees sucking cock. And if it comes to a showdown between who the liar is between you and me, who you think they're gonna believe?"

I didn't even need to answer that question.

Reece, short for Maurice, was the head of the gang that fought my stepbrother street by street/gutter by gutter for territorial dominance on the estate. They were bitter rivals and now he had the perfect ammunition to humiliate his arch enemy and bring him down. But not before he'd used me, it seemed.

"As long as you're horned up and ready, boy, I might as well put you to good use. He forced me down on my knees and shoved his cock between my lips, without a care for my comfort, blocking my airway, suffocating me as he pushed into my throat. When he withdrew I gasped for breath only to face the brutality of his penetration over and over again.

"Hey, look at me, boy. And smile."

I looked up, too late realizing what he was up to. He'd palmed my mobile out of my jeans back pocket, using the mobile phone camera to click graphic photos of me making a meal of his dick. He busily thumbed text messages to all those in my address book, adding his own contacts I discovered later. I would be lucky to finish blowing Reece before my brother had seen evidence of my disgrace. Once he'd sent the incriminating photo, I thought he might ease off but no such luck; he renewed the vigor with which he fucked my face.

Eventually he succumbed to my skill, even to the point of praising me as he dumped his juicy load, before vanishing in case anyone caught him. Sure, I could identify him as the guy I was blowing but I knew he'd deny it. By the time I'd dressed and hauled my aching body out of the toilet block my phone was buzzing.

It was a text message from Biff. Succinct. *HQ. Now!* He didn't often bother to punctuate his messages so I knew from the exclamation mark this was serious. What I should have done was gone home, packed my bag and left the shithole of a city. Although I was good at living on my wits, in a strange new city wits wouldn't pay for food and lodgings. I was good for nothing in the job department.

I bowed my head and made my way to the gang's headquarters where half a dozen of the guys who could be rounded up at short notice waited for me.

I'd already run a number of explanations through my mind on the walk over, including telling the absolute truth but that would only end up with a gang war and serious injury on both sides, as well as my probable demise. No matter which way I looked at it, my death or injury was on the cards. I'd seen the way they'd treated other gay boys on the estate, and I didn't expect any favors because I was Biff's younger half-brother. Exactly the opposite.

He was so purple in the face with anger he was in danger of spontaneous combustion. Unfortunately, that thought made me smile which he interpreted in quite the wrong way. He threw me to the ground and would have kicked me except for the intervention of Zen, his 2IC. He got his nick because he was the only guy who could calm down the gang when their tempers were up. Like now. He'd obviously not had enough time to work his magic or he'd been monumentally unsuccessful as they crowded around me ready to explode.

Biff questioned me through gritted teeth. "Tell me one thing, Red. Tell me you were forced and I'll kill the bastard."

Zen mimed like mad to give Biff the answer he wanted to hear. I'd thought about it. Sure, I admired Biff and in some little sublimated pocket of my libido I acknowledged he was hot, but I was also very tired of his bossing me around, telling me what to do, how to behave, how to live my life.

I sighed. "No, he didn't force me. But I didn't want him taking no pictures neither."

Zen scrunched up his face as if that was the worst possible answer I could have given.

"Doesn't matter, I'll kill the bastard anyway. Who is he?"

I shrugged. "Never seen him before. He's not from around here."

"So you're one of those fuckin' fags that lets any stranger stick his cock in your gob?" His question didn't require an answer so I remained still on the floor. "I bet you swallow, too, right?"

I got angry. "Of course I fuckin' swallow. I may be a fag but I ain't no pussy."

A couple of the guys groaned quietly when I admitted to swallowing. I knew their girlfriends weren't big on oral.

Zen was trying to calm the mood. It was safer to stay on the ground than attempt to stand up and take on my big brother. He was a vicious prick when he was riled.

"You've brought disrespect on the gang, little bro."

"How can I do that when you won't let me join?"

"You're family. And what you do rubs off on us, get it?"

I nodded.

"Someone shows you disrespect, they is showing me disrespect. We can't stand for that. So you gonna tell us who the bastard was who sent this picture?"

"I told ya, he weren't from around here."

"So how come he knew who to send it to?"

"He used my cell phone and just sent it to everyone in my address book."

Biff hopped around on his feet as if the end of the world was just seconds away. "Shit! Shit! Shit! Shit! Shit!"

The gang went into a huddle.

"What the fuck are we gonna do?" my bro asked.

I could see Zen was struggling to find a solution that would save face with the gang and leave me relatively unscathed.

"Why don't we just fuck him over like we do all the fag boys from around here?" one of the guys suggested.

"Better idea," the one named Den smirked. "Why not just fuck him?"

He grinned at the audacity of his suggestion while the others attempted some sort of gross-out look on their face.

"Shit, he lets strangers pork him..." He left it hanging and they filled in the blanks.

I began to crawl away slowly, hoping to reach the door before they made up their mind to my punishment.

"That's pretty sick, bro. Raping the boss's half-brother. Even if he does swallow." I couldn't believe Zen was talking like that. While seeming to talk them out of that particular punishment he was actually reinforcing it. I glared at him. He winked at me. I wanted to jump to my feet and strangle the bastard.

Until I realized, a bit of brutal sex, no matter how sore I was afterwards, was a better outcome than death or serious injury. Victims of gay bashings in the area seldom left hospital in less than two weeks, and then, sometimes permanently damaged.

"Don't that make us fags, too?" a guy asked.

"Nah," Zen said. "You're only a fag if you take it up the butt or swallow a guy's load like pretty boy there."

He was silently sending signals that this was my best chance of survival and to help him out.

I joined in. "Don't even think about it, you sick bastards."

Biff came over and hauled me to my feet, dragging me by the throat to the gang members. "You will pack your bags and be out of the flat by the time I get home this afternoon. If I ever see you around here in the future, I'll kill you. Understand, little bro? Don't think our blood link will save you. It won't."

He pushed me toward the gang and walked away. "Do what you want with him."

Zen held me tightly against his body and whispered in my ear. "Scream, kick, bite, do what you have to but for god's sake don't look like you're enjoying what's about to happen, if you want to come out of this in one piece. Got it?"

I nodded slightly.

Sometimes it was difficult not to enjoy it. They were rough, shoving their cocks at me, eager for release, eager to penetrate. They used my mouth, forcing me to swallow although I railed against the abuse they were showering on my body. Den, impatient for a turn, tore down my jeans and shoved his prick into my ass paving the way for other assaults on my butt. God, it felt so good to have cock in my holes without the barrier of a cubicle wall between me and the man I was servicing. These were guys I'd grown up with, my heroes, and they were fucking me like animals.

Biff was watching from the other side of the club, decidedly uncomfortable because he would often look away or change positions on the stool while he swigged his beer. One or two of the others joined him when they dumped their load, going for refreshment and to recuperate because I thought they were far from finished with me. Without giving me direct credit they were effusive in their praise of the sex, putting it down to the belief they were forcing me to do something I didn't want to do.

I screamed, "You mongrels will rot in hell for what you're doing to me!"

It had the desired effect and they attacked me with more force. Only Zen had remained aloof, merely encouraging the others.

Biff yelled across the club. "Come on, Zen. Get that monster of yours out and really plug the bitch. Make him cry like a fag."

I could see Zen was about to make some excuse but Biff would brook no argument. "Fuck the little fag. Show him what a worthless piece of trash he is. Bust his ass wide open so no one will ever want to fuck him again."

Zen tugged down his jeans while two of the other gang members distracted me, one spewing his cum on my face and one in my ass.

"Hold him, boys," Biff commanded. "He'll try to get away when he gets an eyeful of Zen's wife tamer."

They pinned me down, raising my ass in the air as Zen stood tall. Fuck! His cock was huge, but I was in no doubt I could take it. I'd taken it many times before. When I didn't know who it belonged to. It was one of my regulars. One of my favorite regulars.

I looked into Zen's eyes. I saw that he'd known all along it was me sucking his cock through the wall for all those months. I saw the plea. I went into my act.

"There's no way you're sticking that monster in my ass! Fuck off you twisted bastards. You want to kill me?" I screamed as I struggled to get loose. It was the performance of a lifetime because all I could think of was how much I wanted that cock in my ass where it belonged.

I managed to kick one of the guys holding me and got free until my brother strode across the room and slammed my head down on the floor knocking me senseless for a moment.

When I came round Zen was on top pushing into my ass, fortunately already lubed by two loads that had been dumped up me earlier. He looked me in the eye, apologizing mutely for what he was about to do.

He rammed the full length of his cock past my anal entrance. "Take it you fuckin' fag bitch!" he cried out as I felt his balls slap against my ass cheeks. I sucked in my breath and let out a not entirely faked, "Holy fuck! Take it out! Fuckin' take it out."

Zen must have known that was the worst possible thing he could do. Leaving his cock in my ass until I got used to it was the best solution to the pain I was feeling.

"Take it fag. Feel my hard cock ripping your asshole apart. Never felt anything like it before, have you fag boy?"

That almost did me in. I yelled in pain to disguise the giggle that was threatening to burst out. I sobbed, I pleaded, I cried, anything to get Zen to take his cock out of my ass, all the while holding him in place by squeezing my sphincter around his prick. I wanted to enjoy this buggering, wishing I could get him alone. He picked up the pace once he thought I was comfortable with the size of the weapon lodged inside me.

Zen's humiliating curses, his name calling, and his faux brutality all disguised the fact he was making love to me. I had never felt like this before in my life. My body hummed like a precision musical instrument played by an expert. I lost the will to scream and tapered off to a few grunting noises as if I had lost the will to live, as if all my internal organs had turned to mush. I thought for a while that maybe one of them had. But I had no experience of love or any of the so-called finer emotions.

His movements sped up and I could tell he was close to coming by the words that spewed from his mouth. They excited me as he rubbed his stomach against my hard cock attempting to bring me off at the same time. He didn't have to try too hard as his cock was pushing all the right buttons inside my ass chute. He roared like I have never heard a man roar before. All I could do was suppress a grunt as I felt his cum squirt inside me and I blew my load all over my belly. It squished between us as he collapsed on top of me, my head flopping sideways with the exertion of what we'd both been through.

He licked my ear where no one could see him and whispered his thanks. I wished I could thank him. He kneeled to pull out and I felt cum ooze between my legs before my sphincter snapped shut. I was totally washed out. It was easy to feign unconsciousness.

Den panicked. "Shit! You've fucked him to death."

"Takes more than a coupla cocks to fuck a fag to death," my brother said. "Here. Look."

I felt the splash of warm liquid on my face. He was fucking pissing on me. It went down my nose and burned into the back of my throat. I sat up gasping for breath making it easy for him to aim a stream straight into my mouth. I gulped it down in an attempt to get oxygen into my lungs. By the time he'd finished my eyes were stinging and my hair was soaked in his acrid piss.

Biff intervened. "Lift him up on the table, guys."

I was manhandled across the room to one of the dilapidated wooden tables the club used. Biff followed and ordered that my legs be lifted over my head exposing my ass. He spat in my face, rubbing it over my wet cheeks before plunging three fingers into my mouth.

"Suck on them, slut! Get them nice and slick."

I had an idea what he was thinking of doing and put up a fight. He slapped me hard across the face, stinging my cheeks until tears pooled in my eyes. He didn't have to say a thing.

He pushed two fingers into my gaping asshole.

"You like my fingers in there, bro? All those years I bet you were watching me, just itching to get your faggy mouth round my cock. Eh, bro? Sick fuck." He pushed in and out savagely, adding a third finger, then a fourth. You like cock in your asshole, boy? Yeah, of course, you do. You like the idea of your big brother fisting your butthole?"

"Shit," Den called. "He's got a hard on."

"Sick little fuck!" Biff spat in my face again. I wanted to open my mouth to taste him but I had to keep up the pretense.

"Sick? It's not me has his fingers up his brother's ass," I sneered.

"What? You'd rather it was my cock, pervert boy?"

"You wouldn't dare, you twisted fuck!" I screamed at him.

"Yeah? Try me."

I could see he wanted me to goad him into one of the most taboo of all actions. Truth be told while I was repulsed by the idea I was so turned on I wanted it. Wanted it bad.

"Get your hands off me, bro. You don't want to go down this path. It's totally fucked. Really bad karma."

"He's right," Zen said, thinking my performance was real.

"You're already gonna burn in hell, fag."

"Please don't, I'm begging you," I whimpered. "I'll move away. You'll never see me again. But please don't...fuck me."

He had his cock out, so hard from my total submission to him, pleading for the last shred of my decency, that he could do nothing other than slide into my well-used hole.

The other gang members gasped at the sheer perversity of the action but gradually built up a rhythm chanting, "Fuck him! Fuck him! Fuck him!"

Biff rammed his cock in and out of my butthole. My body tingled at his touch, at the forbidden nature of what he was doing to me. I know he felt it as well. He towered over me. I looked up at him with admiration in my eyes, flexing my ass muscles around his invading prick.

He couldn't stop now even though he knew I was welcoming his thrusts. It took all my willpower not to wrap my legs around his waist, pulling him further inside me. Confusion clouded his face even as he spewed out his four-letter curses, hoping to fuck me to hell. Then disgust took over and he began slapping my face and punching my body, trying to beat the fag out of me. His cry of frustrated rage as he dumped his spunk deep inside me, causing me to squirt for the second time, echoed around the room even as his blows rained down harder than before. Zen ordered the other gang members to pull Biff aside while he bundled me up as best he could and escorted me to the door of the gang HQ.

He whispered to me to get what I could and get out before my brother had time to recuperate and come after me. I quickly pulled my jeans over my slimy body, wiping myself with my shirt. I grabbed my backpack with my cans. They were all my worldly goods. Zen sneaked a fistful of cash into my hand. I mouthed my thanks, regretting I'd never got to know him better, and I got out of there.

I had no need to go back to the desperate flat in which I'd lived. The only remains I left behind were the sprayed paintings I'd created to liven up my bedroom. There was nothing there for which I had any need.

Smelling of sperm, sticky with my brother's spunk and that of his gang, I hitched my way to a city where I could disappear and work my magic on a whole new canvas of streets and alleyways eventually to be discovered, not by the men who paid to use my body, but by men who paid to hang my art in their office buildings and their homes. It took a decade of hard work, of turning around people's perceptions of street art, of promotion by good friends who were art critics and expected nothing of me, so unlike the other leeches I had met through my short life.

I had art dealers beg me for work to hang on their gallery walls. I had men beg to be my boyfriend. None of them lasted more than a few weeks, although fame being the powerful aphrodisiac it is, I was never wanting for sexual partners. But it was all so respectable. So establishment. I was suffocating.

I guess that's why I felt so free sucking cock in the run-down shithouse in the park.

I decided I'd suck one more cock then I would have to join the mayor for the retrospective of my work at the local museum. I was to give a demonstration of my technique, non-sexual alas, and listen to people rabbit on about how the local environment had led to a flowering of my artistic talent. Yeah, right.

I heard the cubicle next to mine open and close and the tell-tale clearing of the throat. I propositioned the intruder with my beckoning finger and shortly a beautiful cock poked its way through the inviting hole. Smiling, I wrapped my lips around the head and put all my effort into bringing him off.

"Oh, my god," he groaned.

I was glad no one else was in the building to hear him.

I slicked his cock, lathering it with my spit as I ran my tongue up and down the shaft, hating to take my mouth off it. I turned and parted my butt cheeks before the inviting prick could be withdrawn, pushing my asshole against the knob feeling it spread wide open by the invading monster. I sighed with satisfaction as I sank back to the wall wishing I could get even more inside me.

I milked the cock hoping to give him the hint to start his own action, tweaking the shaft with my ass muscles.

He gasped again then called tentatively over the partition, "Red? Is that you?"

I chuckled to myself. "Why don't you come in and see for yourself."

My ass felt empty when he withdrew but in seconds he'd pushed open the door and beamed when he saw me. I was surprised that my heart did a little jig when I saw him, too. He wrapped his arms around me and planted the sloppiest kiss on my mouth. When he came up for air, he smiled as he said, "Same old Red. I think I can taste at least two or three loads on your tongue. Don't ever change."

It was good to chat but I wanted to feel him inside me again. Preferably not in a cold dunny stall.

"How about taking me home to finish off what we started," I suggested.

His startled look warned me off. "Unless there's a wife or a boyfriend at home."

"Nah, nothing like that," he blushed. "Sure, why not?"

We pulled our trousers up and looked the height of respectability as we walked across the park to where he lived in a warehouse that he'd converted into a gallery, above which was a living area. It was ramshackle but thriving.

"He was never the same after you left." Zen was explaining about my brother. "It was a couple of years after that...you know. He was getting careless, like he'd lost interest. One of the other gangs ambushed him one night when he was out alone. Did a real good job on him. He never recovered. They turned the machines off at the hospital. Said he was a vegetable. Cops never caught the bastards who did it."

I'd had no word from the old crowd even after I'd made a name for myself. And I'd never revisited the past – until now. Sure, there was a tinge of regret for Biff, but only a tinge. When we reached Zen's new home I could see why he was embarrassed to invite me back. Not only had he salvaged one of my early artworks painted on wood, he'd hung it above the expansive doorway that was the entrance to his gallery, a gallery that he had called Red's.

He looked sheepish. "I'll change it if it's a trade name infringement or if you don't like it," he said.

"Hell, why wouldn't I like it? I'm so flattered."

"I heard you were in town, that's why I went to..."

"Shh. No explanations. Show me around."

He'd built the gallery up from scratch from an old derelict salt warehouse, enlisting the neighborhood to help, as a symbol of their pride in their locality. He'd gathered up local street gang members who showed flare at painting or wood craft or anything even remotely useful, channeling their energy away from the boredom and violence of gang life. You could tell he was a hero to the people working and creating in the safe environment of the gallery. Sure, a lot of the work was mediocre but occasionally pieces showed real flair.

I was effusive in my praise. "I'm so proud of what you've achieved, Zen."

He blushed.

"They'll never be up to your standard, Red, but..." He hesitated. "I'm not proud of what I did that day. Saying sorry is so piss weak after what we did to you."

"You saved my life, that's all."

"I hoped you'd understand the alternative was too terrible to contemplate. But I never meant for Biff, you know..."

"Yeah, I know."

"I wish I could make it up to you."

"You can," I said, suddenly realizing the potential of what had just dropped into my lap. And I didn't just mean the man who I believed I could really come to care for.

"How?"

"Could you rent me some space here to work in? The city is so sterile, I'm losing touch. Maybe I could give your artists a few lessons or pointers. Nothing to tread on your toes, Zen. It's your baby."

"Fuck, that would be so tremendous, man; they look up to you as an inspiration."

"That's not all." I had to choose my words carefully.

"Anything. Name it."

"I'd need somewhere to live while I was here."

"Hell, Red. My place is plenty big enough. Lots of space if you don't mind sharing."

"I don't mind sharing."

"When you think you might like to move in?"

"How about now?"

That spooked him.

"What about your...things?"

"I got all the things I need," I said patting my backpack.

"I think I can get my hands on a second-hand bed quick smart. I'll clean out the spare room and we can set it up—"

I put my finger to his lips.

"What's wrong with your bed?"

I hoped I was not being too forward.

"You'd...are you...what about..."

"When you can string a sentence together, Zen. I don't snore, I don't hog the blankets, but I do have one very nasty habit which may render the whole idea null and void."

Zen looked stricken. "What is it?"

"I need to be fucked, and fucked hard, on a regular basis. Preferably by a very large dick."

"Phew," he said. "That's okay. I think I know where to get one of those."

I patted his crotch as he led me upstairs to my new home.

THE DEX FACTOR

The noise was deafening. A combination of porn, rock music, and real live fucking, I heard it before the lift doors parted on my level. Worse, when the elevator doors opened, I realized the sound was blasting from my own apartment. Even worse, my door was ajar enabling me to make out every word and every sound of porn actors fucking. Plus Arnie, my sleazy next-door neighbor, was getting an eyeful of whatever was going on in my living room.

Worst of all, it sounded as if there were two people attempting to match the crap dialogue and panting in real life. Just as well the McManuses in number two were away visiting their children for a couple of weeks and that there were only three apartments on each level.

Arnie must have heard the ping of the lift as the doors opened for he turned to face me, not at all guilty about being discovered peeping. He smiled lasciviously as my gaze dropped involuntarily to his groin where this thick sausage shape snaked down his shorts, the knob and about an inch of shaft poking out the leg. If I'd been a cock man I guess I would have been impressed, but I'm not. I'd been bailed up once too often by Arnie or his boyfriend Slava, and invited in for a cup of coffee and a blow job. Or even worse.

Both of them were street trash, feral types, with piercings in their nose and ears. Arnie was also inked with animal stripes down his torso. He was the better built of the two, while Slava, being Eastern European, was chunky and dark. They had the annoying habit of running their hands across my chest and over my butt. I told them in no uncertain terms to cut it out but my anger merely emboldened them. One of these days…

"Quite a show in there," Arnie smirked, "Maybe you'd better come into my place until it blows…over."

I couldn't restrain my sarcasm. "Tempting as that offer is, Arnie, I think I'll pass and take my chances at home."

Pushing open my front door, I'd taken a step when Arnie warned, "Watch where you're walking on the tiles in the hallway, I had a little spillage while I was watching the action. All you need is a damp cloth."

I ground my teeth and shut the door loudly in his face. I didn't have to see him to know he would have that superior smirk that was an almost permanent fixture whenever he was around me. True to his word,

I discovered a small puddle of spunk on the tiles where he'd obviously blown a load while perving on…

Well, I'm not gay but it was quite a sight to enter my own living room to be confronted with Dex, seated ministerially on the lounge, his eyes glued to the flat screen TV on which a gang of toughs were gang fucking two blondes who seemed to be thoroughly enjoying the experience. So was the blonde between Dex's legs, happily slurping on his engorged cock. I grabbed the remote to turn down the sound. Only then did he acknowledge my presence while holding the girl's head down on his prick.

"That's it, honey, lick my balls." Turning to me, he added. "I like your taste in porn, man. Very hot. Does my sis know what sort of heavy shit you watch to get your rocks off when she's not around?"

"Where did you get those movies?" I demanded.

"In your bedroom. In a drawer, under your underwear."

"Don't you ever go into my bedroom again," I said calmly, raging silently inside.

"If your bedroom's private you should lock the door," he mocked. "I bet Lisa doesn't know about your little stash, does she?"

"None of your business," I huffed.

"I know she doesn't like porn. Thinks it's degrading to women. God alone knows what she'd think of this kinky shit."

Dex's companion took no notice of our conversation, instead concentrating on sucking his cock. He saw me looking at her.

"Melanie's a Grade A cocksucker. You should give her a go. I can see you'd like to." He nodded at my erection, obvious in my tight trousers. Yeah, I admit, it was hot seeing the porn again. It had lain neglected in the drawer for months now because of Lisa's derisory attitude to all things cinematically sexual. That, plus the fact Melanie was a looker, was enough to make a grown man weep. Or, at least a grown man's cock weep, which mine was doing, much to my annoyance.

Dex leaned over the chick deep throating him and dug his fingers into her pussy. It was dripping, whether from his previous exploits or from the anticipation of my joining in, I wasn't sure, but I turned on my heels and slammed into my bedroom, closing the door very tightly on the temptation in the living room.

I flung myself on the bed, unzipping to allow my cock room to breathe. Single-handedly I dialed Lisa. It was a forlorn hope that she'd be up for a bit of phone fun but I could always try, the image of Melanie down on her knees sucking Dex's rather impressive prick all the way down her throat meant I was in dire need of relief. I'd heard rumors about Dex's prodigious talent in the crotch department but, until now, I had no way of knowing whether the matter between his legs was formidable or otherwise.

Now I knew that it was.

"Hi, honey," Lisa purred down the phone, immediately reinvigorating my cock. "I miss you."

That's what I loved about Lisa: the way she doesn't just speak, she coos, wrapping you in the warm embrace of her voice. It made my heart jump, as well as my dick. At work, I'm a ruthless bastard, known for my cut-throat take-no-prisoners approach to takeovers and mergers. But Lisa turns me into a pussy. That's how I got saddled with Dex in the first place. I knew it wouldn't work but she insisted, in that soft but seductive way she has, that I take in her recalcitrant brother, newly released from a low-level security prison for minor crimes he maintains he didn't commit. Lisa later confided, one night when she'd gone over the very meager limit of her alcohol tolerance, that he had actually committed the crimes and, in fact, had done much worse.

Dex was a mercenary bastard, but smart with it. He knew enough not to be seen reverting to his previous grubby behavior while his big sis was around, actually ingratiating himself with me to the extent that I thought the rumors about his behavior had to be lies. He was helpful around the apartment, went out of his way to give me my personal space, never interfering in my day-to-day living. He also went overboard to make me his buddy. I was too astute to confide secrets to him, but he knew from Lisa's description that some of my personal habits were not to her liking. They were definitely to his. My drug and alcohol intake, for example, which I had curtailed reluctantly at Lisa's behest. Until she arrived in my life I had liked to work hard and party harder.

Dex was also seductive in the manner in which he shared confidences about his appalling behavioral lapses with which he knew I would sympathize. In reality, he was a pimp. He pimped friendship, sexual favors, people, as well as party favorites. He had charm to spare. He also had the advantages of education, good looks, a pretty impressive body, albeit almost totally hairless except for a ridge atop his equally impressive prick. He also had a mouth that made my cock twitch, not that I would ever tell him that. His lips were full, sensuous, cunt-like, his tongue often licking along them as if in open invitation. I often thought he was deliberately provoking me to see how far I'd go. Not that far, mate.

I'd already been in Lisa's bad books when I'd crashed and burned at various parties in my hedonistic pursuit of prescription or alcoholic oblivion and, once or twice, conquered the wrong pussy. News of my conquests always got back to Lisa. I'd received my third, and final, warning. Next slip-up, our relationship was over. I'd been good for months and it was killing me, but I'd kept my fly zipped, my mouth locked, and my libido imprisoned. If I didn't know Lisa did not have a devious bone in her body, I would have accused her of leaving me at enticement's door by going away for a month. Dex was temptation incarnate.

Not that she believed, like I did, that her little brother was Satan himself. She knew he'd got in with the 'wrong crowd' and his behavior was less than exemplary but she was not privy to the fine print of it like I was. I knew the uncensored Dex. And yet, I still liked the bastard.

It was only after Lisa went back to the country town where she was born, to look after her dad, as her mum was recovering from a near fatal illness that kept her bedridden, unable to look after her husband, that I began to see flashes of the evil within him. Lisa believed my time alone with Dex was the ideal opportunity for us to 'bond' – like brothers. I didn't like to spoil her fantasy by pointing out most brothers I know are highly competitive and loathe one another.

The day she left, Dex morphed into his true shape. The monster he'd kept on a leash while Lisa was around suddenly burst out with all the vigor of a creature that had been suppressed too long. I'd been told of his excesses, now I was experiencing them first-hand. They barely affected me apart from the unsavory types he invited back to my apartment for god-knew-what, although the noise bothered me. I needed my sleep in order to perform well at my job. There were younger, more aggressive, more ambitious salespeople baying at my heels, including my best mate, Chris, whose elevation was stymied every step of the way by my success.

I told Lisa none of this as we whispered sweet love down the phone, me wrapping my hand around my cock while thinking how good it would feel buried up to my balls in Melanie's twat. God, how I ached for it. Sure, I loved Lisa, but she wasn't here to relieve the ache. If only Dex wasn't such a caring, sharing individual. If only he hadn't offered Melanie's services.

I was ruthless, yes, but with the willpower of a daffodil when it comes to pleasure. I was making such soothing sounds to Lisa because since she'd left it had taken only a matter of days for me to break down and join Dex in his whirlwind debaucheries. Okay, it was mainly drugs and booze with the occasional knob polishing from one of his girls, but it meant nothing. It was relieving pure animal need. Lisa should have known better than to leave me here at the mercy of my addictions. And the manipulations of her brother.

It had begun with me buying speed from him to get through the days at work without sleep. It rapidly progressed from there until I was as much in his debt as I ever could be but still manage to wriggle my way out of his influence. I had to trust him because he had his hand around my nuts, metaphorically speaking, and could squeeze any time he wanted. I knew he wouldn't though. I was pretty sure he wanted to see me married to his big sis.

I teased Lisa. "I have a very important question to ask you when you get back."

"What is it?" she asked excitedly.

She'd badgered me for ages about making our relationship official, but I'd always baulked at losing my freedom. But Dex had shown me I could have a marriage and indulge myself as well. It would take some nifty footwork but I could do it. Plus, I was feeling incredibly guilty. This was a sop to my conscience. I'd consider the consequences later. That's what laters were for.

"Please, Jude, what is it?"

"It's not the sort of question a person asks over the phone."

She squealed so loudly I had to hold the phone away from my ear.

There was nowhere to go with the conversation after that so we swapped a few lovey doveys, promising eternal fidelity, and I rang off, feeling not the slightest guilt now that I hoped Melanie was still available. I heard Dex's distinctive ring tone in the next room. Lisa was predictable. She was obviously ringing her brother to tell him I had all but proposed, it was just a matter of setting the date.

Not wishing to interrupt the call, I remained in my room, stroking my dick just managing to keep ejaculation at bay. The door opened quietly, Dex's voice loud with pleasure at the news, as Melanie slipped into the room. She was naked, crawling up the bed until her head was level with my crotch. She peeled my hand off my cock and took me in her mouth. I exhaled deeply, surrendering myself to her expert mouth. On the odd occasion that Lisa had reluctantly taken me orally, she had done so with such ill grace and such abhorrence I knew she was doing it as a sop to save her pussy after reeling me in as a prospective husband, parsimonious in handing out sexual relief until after the wedding. She had captured me with her delightful inexperience, making a play of innocence, content to let me believe that more fulsome delights awaited the marriage bed.

But her pathetic attempts to relieve me orally, spitting the results into a tissue she held in her hand during the entire operation – I call it an 'operation' because she attacked the task with all the finesse of a military maneuver, and none of the spontaneity of desire. I knew that once the ring was on her finger she would not be giving me head. It couldn't be bitterness that I did not return the favor because I ate her pussy with all the energy and appetite of a man starving for the flavor. I usually managed to bring her off at least twice but her distaste was obvious. I do believe she thought the role of sex should be confined to marriage and then only to procreate.

I was vain enough to believe that once she got a taste of what I could unleash, she would be eager to accommodate my cock in any of her various orifices I desired. Needless to say, her anal virginity was sacrosanct.

You can see then why I groaned my appreciation of Melanie's expert oral ministrations. I was disappointed when she removed her lips, and throat, from my prick but only for as long as it took her to squat over my rigid shaft and impale her tight, wet pussy to the hilt. I reached up to tweak her nipples, another of Lisa's dislikes: "Don't Jude, that hurts."

My future wife had no concept of the principle of pain/pleasure. And had no inclination to learn. I would instruct her. Melanie needed no such schooling, grinding her cunt down onto my balls, gripping my prick in her steaming tunnel, eager to milk every drop of my juice. Bucking helplessly as she used all her skills to bring me to climax, I exploded inside her, shooting wad after wad of spunk deep in her pussy as she screamed her own orgasm, finally slumping against my chest.

It was only then I noticed Dex standing in the doorway leering, his mobile phone raised to shoot video footage of our action. I was so depleted, it did not strike me as unusual behavior. It seemed a harmless enough pastime given our perverse natures.

I fell into one of the soundest sleeps I had managed since Lisa had gone to the country, fortunate that the next day was Saturday. It was almost noon when I staggered out of the bedroom to brew coffee to start the day, Melanie obviously having left at some point after we'd had our fun. My head was fuzzy from too much sleep, you know that feeling like your head is full of cotton wool? It was okay though, I had nothing planned, except to relax and go with the party mood that Dex would have planned. His weekend orgies of excess were legendary to everyone except Lisa. Although I was on the periphery – by choice – I still managed to have more fun than most poor suckers ever dreamed of in a lifetime. I was careful in case gossip got back to Lisa, but Dex was not likely to tell because she had threatened him with sisterly excommunication if she heard he'd reverted to his old ways. We covered for each other.

The delicious smell of coffee brought Dex out in his fashion underwear which hugged the curve of his ass and the contour of his prick which was either well on the way to erection or else was a shower not a grower. He scratched his balls unashamedly.

"Melanie want a coffee?" I asked.

"She left around midnight. Had to get home to her husband. Stupid bastard suspects nothing even when she fucks him with a cunt full of other men's spunk. What a loser!"

"What you got planned for the weekend?"

Dex put his arm around my shoulders. I could feel the heat from his body through my T-shirt, plus the odor of stale sweat and sex that was strangely erotic. "What I've got planned is beyond your wildest dreams, mate. So just relax and go with it and I guarantee it will be like nothing you've ever experienced before."

Any reaction from me was redundant but I felt obliged to mutter, "Cool."

"Who knows," he laughed. "You might even enjoy it."

It was a strange thing to say but before I could query him on the matter, he went on. "So, Lisa tells me you intend popping the question when she returns."

"Yeah," I replied. "It's time I settled down, got a family started."

"You think you're good enough for her?" he asked.

It seemed an innocent joke but I detected an undercurrent to his voice. My answer was a laugh as I didn't think it warranted anything more, but Dex gripped my shoulder tighter. "Maybe you should have asked me first."

I was so surprised I just blurted out, "Why would I do that?"

"She's family. I want to see the right thing done by her."

"You're close enough to know if I'm suitable," I said in an attempt to keep it light although I was pissed off at his attitude.

He finally released me, helping himself to a mug of coffee. "She can't marry just anybody."

"I'm not just anybody," I protested.

He relaxed, spreading himself out on the lounge. "You're right. You're not just anyone."

He found the remote control and turned on the television, simultaneously firing up the DVD player which sprang to life mid-scene of a heavy gangbang bisexual porn. This gang was working over some chick while her boyfriend or husband was forced to watch from a chair to which he was bound. There were too many men for the chick to accommodate at once and a few of the guys hovered around the bound cuckold eyeing him up as a prospective cum dump.

We watched in silence for a while until my initial disgust turned to excitement as the chick's boyfriend was released, stripped, and manhandled to the ground where he became a slut for the gang's cocks and spooge. It was difficult to disguise my reaction as I was in shorts. Dex made no attempt to hide his obvious erection, stroking it through his jockeys.

"You like?" he whispered.

I had to clear my throat to answer. "Not bad."

He drew a small bottle from his briefs, unscrewed the cap, and held it to his nose.

Poppers. The poor man's drug of choice. Instant high, but of short duration. No lasting side effects except the occasional headache. Fags popularized it as a disco drug in the 1970s. I'd used it sparingly when I was younger. I was surprised Dex was a user.

"Oh, man, that is so hot," he groaned, handing me the bottle as he released his dick.

Somewhere at the back of my mind was the nagging question as to whether this was some sort of perverse test, none the less, I took a few deep sniffs and waited for the buzz. It almost blew my head off. It was much stronger than the shit I'd used before.

"Hospital strength," Dex smiled. "The real shit, not that rubbish they sell in sex shops. Good, eh?"

I had to agree. I was flying. I yanked out my cock, all moral qualms extinguished. I was hard and I wanted satisfaction.

Dex kept up a running commentary on what a slut the guy was to allow himself to be abused sexually. "Look at the way the fag sucks cock. Like a true believer," Dex gloated. "You ever let a fag suck your cock, Jude?"

"Nah, I don't do that shit."

"Nasty. Look at the way they're fucking his mouth, spunk all over his face, making him swallow. Bet that gets you so fuckin' hard."

Yeah, it did. What the fuck was the matter with me?

I was still holding on to the poppers. "Go on, take another hit. It'll really blow you away."

I did it without thinking as the porn action switched from the chick back to her boyfriend. I concentrated on the screen so intently I didn't hear Dex move until I felt a warm mouth around my prick. It was like all the feelings in my body were increased tenfold. I felt Dex's warm wet lips, the ones I'd fantasized about. I felt his tongue, and then I felt his throat constrict around my shaft. Part of me wanted to push him away but the drug had lowered my resistance until all I wanted was that magnificent face embedded around my prick. I grabbed the back of his head and fucked him until he sounded as if he were choking. I didn't let up until I blew my load down his gullet. He swallowed every drop. It was not a case of like brother like sister.

"Oh, fuck, I've never done that before," I wheezed.

"Intense, eh?"

"Fuck, yeah!"

Dex sat back on the lounge next to me, dragging my hand to his prick, obviously wanting me to help him out.

"I don't do that," I said.

He didn't turn surly or anything like that. He merely said, "Fair's fair. It's your turn. Stop thinking about it. Just do it. Take another hit."

I supposed giving him a hand job wouldn't kill me, after all, he'd blown me. Better than Melanie. Much better than Lisa.

To put my morals to sleep I took a giant hit in both nostrils and began to jerk his cock. Once the fumes hit the blood stream it was easy enough for Dex to maneuver me to the floor between his legs to insert his cock into my mouth. I was too spaced out to resist. I looked up at him hoping he'd read my reluctance and let me go.

I looked into the eyes of pure fuckin' evil.

"Suck it, you fuckin' slut," he spat. He held my head in place so I could not escape, but I was so drug fucked I continued to follow his orders. He shoved the bottle under my nose after taking a snort of his own.

His face screwed up into a gargoyle of pure feral trash. I knew if I were to survive this I needed all the help I could get. I sniffed. Sniffed again just in time as he plugged my mouth and throat with his enormous cock as puke slime ran out of my nose and mouth. He slut fucked my face until I thought I would pass out, all the time cursing me for the slut I was.

"You like it, boy? You like sucking my big hard cock?"

He let me loose to answer, my face covered with saliva and tears. "Yes," I said, knowing it was what he wanted to hear.

"I can't hear you," he said maliciously.

While I was enduring the abuse, the porn movie echoing our own dialogue, part of my brain was actually enjoying the experience. I would later justify that on the grounds that I was being forced into the, to me, alien activity.

Right now though, I just wanted it all to be over. "I love sucking your huge stiff cock, Dex," I yelled. "I can't get enough of it. Fuck my slut mouth. Spew your cum all over my face and down my fuckin' throat."

"With pleasure, you whore!"

He dumped a load, holding my head, forcing me to swallow. The taste wasn't all that unpleasant, it wouldn't kill me. Then he released me and I could breathe again.

"You bastard," I snarled.

He smiled. "Calm down. You may be angry now but I bet this afternoon you jerk off thinking about what we just did. Accept it and move on."

"You set me up!" I cursed.

"Of course, I did. Just like you set up any chick you want to fuck. The whole world does it. What's the big deal? I sucked you. You reciprocated. We're mates. It's what mates do."

"Not this mate!"

I stormed off into my bedroom, slamming the door as he yelled after me, "See if I'm not right."

The bastard was right.

After I calmed down, I replayed the action in my mind. No one was hurt, I'd blown a load. Admittedly,

Dex had used more force than I thought was necessary. And he was a devious bastard. But…

I didn't want to know about any buts.

My cock needed attention so, eventually, I capitulated, wanking myself to orgasm over the memory of what we'd just done.

After a shower and shave, I emerged from my funk. Dex watched my reaction carefully before his face broke into a huge smile. "I was right, wasn't I?"

"Fuck you," I said, but I was grinning.

"Mates?"

"Mates."

Grudges are useless, so I let mine go, after all, there was the promise of a great night ahead and some fine female ass. Neither Dex nor I were the cleaning type, I have a woman come in once a week, so we just stored breakables in drawers and cupboards in preparation for a wild party. With the MacManuses away and the sleaze boys next door peeping through the open front door we were unlikely to have problems with the neighbors. Perhaps the gay residents below may object to the sound of music whoofing through their ceiling but Dex paid them a visit and plied them with copious amounts of wine and free tickets to the theatre. I suspect now there may also have been a bit of reciprocal cock sucking and ass licking to sweeten the deal. They were more than amenable to turning a deaf ear to our activity.

Dex was still promising something special but refused to tell me what it was.

"You'll just have to wait," he kept repeating.

It started out as something special. There was a real buzz to the party, an equal mix of hot young chicks and hot young studs, no one over early thirties by my calculations, and all up for any depravity Dex could conjure. The surprise was the quality ice he'd managed to buy from his dealer, assuring us of the most intense high of all time. I'd done meth before but tended to stay away because of its addictive qualities. The feelings it engendered were so amazing, the more you wanted to repeat them. That way lay disaster.

Some of the heavy users and abusers injected in the bathroom while the rest of us inhaled from the glass pipes that Dex so thoughtfully supplied. I warmed the bowl, inhaling the vapor from the green-tinged crystals. Within minutes, euphoria overwhelmed me, my confidence, not slight at the best of times, knew no bounds, my awareness peaked. I was ready to fuck the world.

I'm not sure where the time went but my cock was almost raw by midnight when I collapsed in a heap along with a herd of hard-core partygoers. People had come and gone, in both senses of the words, during the night, strangers as well as friends, but I didn't care. As long as there were holes to plug with my rampant cock, I was happy. Clothes were discarded in a sexual free-for-all, people fucking and sucking in any gender or numerical combination on the floor, on the beds, even on the balcony which would probably get a nasty rebuke from nosy neighbors.

Somewhere during the night, I'd rung my best mate, Chris, to come on over. We might be mates but we shared little outside our work environment and in my drugged state I thought this was an opportunity to bond. That's how really drug fucked I was. He did turn up and he joined in the riot of excess. Mark one up for friendship.

I remember I was starting to come down from my high around midnight, collapsing on my bed, hoping to sleep in order to ward off the heebie-jeebies I knew weren't far away. It must have been the early hours of the morning when I awoke, the apartment eerily quiet although I could hear the pulse of the bass line to the music coming from the CD speakers, my room so dark I could see the strip of light from the living room underneath my door.

It was the feel of soft lips around my cock that woke me. I never thought I'd be ready to go again, but I was hard. I'd thought I was dreaming but the suction was real. God, it was real. I pushed my groin up into the willing mouth, reaching to push the head down to my balls.

Fuck! I recoiled in horror, attempting to kick the head and the body away from me. I leaned over to turn on the bedside light. Tell me it wasn't so. Slithering up the bed to reattach its foul mouth to my prick was Arnie, his great gash of a mouth slobbering at the thought of finally getting to taste my spunk.

"Fuck off, Arnie!" I yelled, trying to find something to throw at him. "I don't do that."

"Oh, really?" he said, sounding like some vicious street queen. "Then I suppose that movie on your TV is all fake?"

"What movie?"

"You chowing down on Dex's meat, begging to be his whore."

"What the fuck!"

Arnie chuckled. "You are a dark horse."

I stood up quickly, almost falling over my trousers which were down around my ankles. I yanked them up, attempting to retain some dignity, slamming my way into the living room. There were scarcely a dozen people remaining, all in various stages of undress. Dex was using his mobile phone to film a young couple fucking in the corner. She was wearing a strap-on, plundering her partner's ass while he screamed for it harder.

As I emerged there was a scattering of applause from those watching TV, including Chris. I was horrified to see myself on the screen, down on my knees sucking Dex, begging to be used. He'd obviously set up a camera in anticipation of getting me to pleasure him. Whether his ultimate aim was my humiliation or for blackmail I was unsure but it would be difficult to keep it a secret after this lot were finished. Some of them were using their own phones to grab a screen shot.

"The butterfly emerges from his cocoon," Dex said. "Welcome, Jude. Only the real serious partygoers are still here. The evening is young, the excitement has only just begun."

I was feeling lethargic, despondent. I was in need of another hit. Dex saw my plight.

"Need an energy boost, Jude? Be my guest." He handed me a syringe.

"Uh, where's the pipe?"

"The guests were very clumsy. All broken. Anyway, you're among friends here. Heavy duty party fuckers. This will get into your system quicker."

Dex was an expert. Before I even had time to consider what he was doing, the meth was coursing through my body. I relaxed. I was amongst friends. Even Arnie and Slava were my pals. They were still my mates as they roughly removed my clothes, forced me onto the coffee table and lifted my legs, rubbing something sticky on my asshole. It felt good but I didn't want this.

"Hold him," Dex commanded.

He rubbed a cream on his cock which was red and swollen, aimed it between my butt cheeks, and pushed. Sure, there was pain but it didn't seem to be happening to me. He rammed away at my hole, spreading my sphincter wide open as he pounded me. It was pain/pleasure. He looked me in the eye, his face contorted with hatred. "My sister is too good for the likes of you, cunt boy. You'll never have her."

He kept up a litany of obscenities while he drove his prick deep inside, his face revealing all the festering evil. The horrifying part of it, I was so turned on I never wanted it to end. It was like the universe was in my ass and I wanted to be fucked forever.

"You will be," he said. "When I put the word out that your ass is for hire, there will be a line around the block. We'll make a fortune out of you, slut. You'll be on your back day and night until your ass is so clapped out no one will want you any more, not even the drunken pimps in smelly shithouses."

"Go on, do it!" I spat at him. "I'm a fuckin' whore. That's all I deserve. I want cock and cum until I can't stand up."

He laughed at me. He slapped my face. Hard. "You're my slut now, fucker. You'll beg me to slam your asshole. You'll get down on a pissy bathroom floor and suck cock until you puke."

I knew I would do it, too. Dex obviously intended to get me hooked on meth so that I'd do anything to get a fix. My only hope was Chris. If I could just get him alone, he could save me.

There was a fragment of my brain still functioning but it was overwhelmed by the pleasure that engulfed my body making me feel invincible.

Dex pulled out. "Who's next?"

Slava elbowed other takers aside and rammed his stubby cock up my butt.

"Fuck me hard. I want to feel you," I whispered to him. I saw Arnie loom up, yanking my head back to bury his prick in my mouth. The two of them fucked me simultaneously. I wanted to see the ugly cunt fucking my ass but it was impossible with Arnie choking me. Still I could feel Slava's cock opening my hole wide. He had no regard for me, I was just a hole in which to relieve himself and he unloaded pretty quickly. Arnie immediately took his place. That was better. I could see his features as he tormented me, pinching my nipples, squeezing my balls as he sank his cock inside me.

The spunk in my ass squelched as Arnie shoved in and out, adding a degenerate sound to the proceedings. I hoped Dex was capturing it all on video. I'd want to relive this moment over and over. Arnie gobbed a mouthful of spit in my face to show his contempt, probably for the miserable way I'd treated them in the past. I didn't care. It made my punishment all the more enjoyable.

The piercings on his face took on a subhuman luster, the stripes tattooed on his body adding a dangerous animal element.

I heard a voice begging Arnie to tear my ass open, fill it with spunk, and I realized it was me. I was losing the struggle to stay on top of the game.

I squeezed my ass muscles around Arnie's dick. Why hadn't I thought of that before, instead of just lying passively taking cock? His eyes flew open in surprise and he muttered a string of profanities as I brought him to climax. He pulled out, shaking his dribbling cock over my stomach.

I wondered how I could talk to Chris without arousing suspicion. I knew his regard for me as a mate would save me. I was certain most of the party would take a turn at my ass. If I could get them off quickly then I still had a chance.

Unexpectedly, Chris loomed up in my line of sight.

"Mate," I whispered.

He leaned forward to listen to what I had to say.

I had to concentrate harder than I ever had before to form the words, to make my mouth speak. "You've got to help me. Got to get me out of here."

His smile reassured me, then his face contorted into rage and I felt his cock at my guts. He pushed into me just like the others, grabbing my throat, squeezing it painfully. He looked like hate personified as he cursed me, flinging his contempt for me in my face.

"You think you're so fuckin' superior, don't you? No one likes you, Jude. We all think you're an asshole. Can't wait for you to take a fall. Tonight you have. Big time. Wait till the guys at the office get a load of the video of you being a cock slut. I guess they'll be lining up to show you what they really think of you as well. Your ass is sweet, baby, you were born to be fucked. I'll make sure I plug you every chance I get. Breed your ass."

My cock was so hard I thought it would burst apart as Chris fucked me. It didn't last nearly long enough. After he blew his load, he wiped his slimy prick across my face, ordering me to lick it clean.

His parting shot sent a chill through me. "Don't bother turning up for work on Monday. I'll make sure the entire staff gets a good look at you in action, mate. You won't dare show your face."

The rest of the party took turns tapping my ass, including the chick with the strap-on, continuing long after my ass and my throat hurt like I'd been run down by a bulldozer. Still they kept coming. Somewhere during the assault, I was allowed to go to the bathroom to expel the contents of my ass and my stomach. Then it was back to the unrelenting grind of cocks and cum.

Time ceased to have any meaning for me. My life revolved around cocks. Sure, Dex allowed breaks for showers and food, not that I felt like eating, but most of the time I was flat on my back or my stomach taking cock in my ass and my throat. I watched emotionlessly as Dex took money from strangers at the door. The men all blurred into one another although I was sure I saw Arnie and Slava on more than one occasion and I know Chris returned over and over because his voice was so distinctive in its contempt. He brought other guys who worked at my office and they made a party of my body, egging each other on until my ass gaped and spunk oozed out of me like a slimy creek.

I had no idea whether days, weeks or months passed. All I knew was the constant craving for meth, and then I would have to get down on my hands and knees and beg Dex to relieve my pain. He did but only after I had debased myself even further, drinking his piss, licking his ass like I was human toilet paper.

Then one day through the fog of my drugged brain, I heard Lisa's voice. Snatches of conversation. "What's going on here? What have you done to Jude?"

followed by Dex's accusation, "He wasn't good enough for you."

"You don't think anyone is good enough for me!"

If I hoped for salvation I was cruelly disappointed. I felt a needle prick while the argument raged before Dex brought Lisa over to watch while Arnie made me beg him to fuck me.

I saw the look of horror on Lisa's face as the full import of my battered and slimy body hit home. Her disgust was palpable. Then the meth hit home and I no longer cared about anything but the pleasure in my ass.

I don't know how long the drug-induced stupor lasted except that when I emerged, I could no longer hear Lisa. It was too much to hope she had gone for help. A sort of sex haze fogged my brain. I couldn't quite make out who was pounding my ass, all I knew was he gave me no human consideration as he behaved like an animal, cursing me, telling me how much I deserved to be fucked and humiliated. I knew the voice but my fuddled brain could not put a name to it. I didn't care.

I was face down on the coffee table again, only this time it was shaking from another person being brutally fucked beside me. I recognized Dex's voice reveling in his profanities telling the bitch she was his to do as he liked.

"You'll beg me to fuck you. I'm the only man who will ever truly satisfy you," he boasted.

I squeezed my spunk-encrusted eyelids open, peering at the face across the coffee table from mine. It was as drug-fucked blank as mine probably was, her mind a thousand miles away from the depravity being committed on her body. The face was Lisa's. Dex was pounding her ass, that same ass she would never surrender to me.

I closed my eyes, none of it mattered any more. Lisa was a thing of the past. I had a new love now to take care of me, wrap me in her loving arms. Her name is Lady Ice.

JAILHOUSE COCK

What woke me up was the prick to my throat. Not that sort of prick. One that drew blood. I felt the warm trickle down my chest.

"Where is she, cunt?"

I wasn't at all surprised to wake up, my life threatened. I'd never felt safe in this room. What did surprise me was opening my eyes to stare up into the snarling face of a shaven-headed bastard, his eyes full of murderous intent. Nor did I expect my cock to get hard when I briefly glimpsed his huge biceps and the do-it-yourself tattoos along his arms.

"Where the fuck is she?" he screamed, his spit landing on my face.

I had no idea what he was talking about.

A sixth sense had warned me not to take this ground-floor boarding house room, but it was all I could afford. There were few alternatives: I could succumb and move into a communal apartment or house share with a number of other impecunious student types like myself. Or I could go back home and live with my parents. Neither alternative appealed. I like my privacy. The room itself was fine, although the furnishings were Spartan: a three-quarter bed, a wardrobe and chest of drawers, what more could a poor student want apart from the share kitchen and a very unsavory share bathroom and toilet at the end of the hall? Well, there was the airy side window that flooded the room with light. That was the problem. The window. It just happened to be on the ground floor. It was invisible from the street because it was down a passageway shielded by a rotting wooden gate that was permanently locked. From the backyard, a number of leafy bushes edged the passage mouth. It was an ideal entrance for anyone with mischief on his or her mind.

The real estate agent assured me they'd never had any break-ins but I learned later he'd been somewhat casual with the truth. True, no one had ever broken into the four-story building since it had become a boarding house aimed at the student and musician market but there had been one murder – unsolved, three suicides, five overdoses, two dozen thefts, and a partridge in a pear tree. The list of tragedies was so long it might just as well have been a Christmas carol.

But no break-ins. That meant all the other mayhem had been inside jobs. I quickly installed a deadlock on the only door even though it was against house rules and could get me thrown out. As an added measure, I drilled screw holes in the window frames so the bottom window would open only far enough that an arm could intrude. No way was a human body gonna fit through that space. I suppose I should have taken all those precautions from day one but, hell, security costs money and that was something I did not have in great abundance.

At least I slept calmly once the locks and bolts were in place. Big mistake. I woke up a hair's breadth from death, choking for breath, a grip of iron about my throat. The shaved-headed snarling belligerent whose face was inches from my own had substituted throttling for throat slitting. Less blood, I guessed.

"Okay, fucker!" he spat. "Where is she?"

If he actually wanted an answer rather than drowning me in his saliva, he'd have to let me go. I'm sure by now I was purple in the face, not my most attractive coloring, and certainly in danger of passing out. He must have realized and released me. I gasped for air, taking huge gulps into my lungs. As my heart slowed marginally, from thumping fit to burst out through my ribs to merely fluttering, I looked at my tormentor.

Yep, he was precisely the sort of reason I didn't want to live at home and share with other students. This guy was hot in a way that meant if I had to die, a victim of murder, this is the kind of guy I would prefer to do it.

One of his gobs oozed down my cheek. My tongue snaked out to taste it. Salty mucous. I rolled it around on my tongue, and then swallowed it down. If the intruder saw me he gave no indication.

My throat felt like sandpaper when I rasped out, "Where's who?"

"Don't come the dumb cunt with me," he snapped. "If I find out you're fuckin' her, I'll cut you up so fine they'll mistake your body parts for sushi."

"Okay, look. My name is Luke. I'm a student. I moved in here six months ago. I don't know who was here before me, I didn't ask, but I have been getting these letters addressed to a Kylie. Is that who you're looking for?"

"Where are the letters?"

I got up slowly, but still he sprang back in case I was about to attack him, raising the knife to chest level. "I kept them in case this Kylie chick called in to pick them up. I was gonna give it a few more weeks then mark them Return to Sender. They're on the table over there." He sat at my cheap laminated table and ill-matching chairs, keeping a wary eye on me as he spread the envelopes out in front of him.

"Don't try anything fucker because I'll be on to you before you even reach the door."

He began searching through the pile, muttering threats. "If I find some other fucker has been writing to her he's dead meat."

I knew there was only one writer as all the correspondence was in the same handwriting and it was all marked from Long Bay Jail.

"You wrote those letters?"

"What's it to you?" he said.

I shrugged. "How'd you get in here anyway?"

He snorted his derision. "You really think a couple of screws in a window frame as old as this shit heap could withstand a bit of force?"

I examined the window and saw the deep scour marks where the nails had splintered through the rotting window jamb. So much for security. I went and sat opposite the guy.

"You sure she's not here?" he asked, sounding thoroughly defeated.

"Take a look around. You see anything that looks even remotely like a chick lives here?"

He rifled through my closet and my drawers.

"Not that drawer," I yelled.

He smirked, thinking he was about to find proof that his Kylie was my secret lover.

"Why not? Scared I might find something incriminating?"

He wrenched the drawer out spilling the contents on the floor, jumping back in surprise.

"What the fuck?"

"I warned you."

"What is that shit?"

"What's it look like?"

"Sex toys."

"Give the man a prize." I went over to gather up the spill and hide it away again but he was too quick for me, grabbing one of the larger dildos.

"You use this on some chick? She must have a cunt like the Grand Canyon." He waved it around like a comedy prop.

Grabbing it from him, I stuffed it back in its hiding place and turned on him. "Listen up. There are no chicks. Not Kylie, not any female. I'm gay. The toys are for me. I like cock up my ass. Got it?"

"You're shittin' me? No way could you fit that up your butt."

"Wanna bet?"

"Must hurt like hell."

"Yeah, well, with that one I need a bit of chemical assistance."

"Uh?"

He was as thick as two planks.

"Drugs."

"You got drugs?" he asked with more enthusiasm than he'd shown so far.

"Nothing much at present. Just poppers."

He seemed disappointed. "Gives me a headache," he said. "Got any grog?"

I opened the small fridge I'd smuggled into my room. Cooking was strictly forbidden anywhere in the boarding house except for the communal kitchen which was so rancid with mold, food scraps and toxic leftovers that even the cockroaches avoided it for fear of contracting food poisoning. Everyone cooked in their rooms which meant we had to put up with the periodic memos slipped under our doors demanding we cease such activity immediately on pain of expulsion. These usually appeared after one of the smoke alarms had been triggered by burning toast. Solution? Simple. Most of us removed the smoke alarm batteries as soon as we moved in.

I handed over a half bottle of Jack Daniels and two glasses. He sat backwards on the chair, at home with my alcohol, glaring at me.

"How long you in the…um… resort?" I asked when the silence was threatening to become lethal. He'd downed two glasses of bourbon which seemed to make him more belligerent than mellow.

"How did you know I…?"

I tapped the return address on the front of his envelopes then poured myself a generous portion of liquor.

It was getting late. "You got anywhere to stay tonight?"

"Halfway house on the other side of the city. But I thought I'd be staying here with Kylie. Didn't expect she'd run out on me."

"If you like, you can stay the night cause it's getting late for public transport."

"I don't trust queers."

"You can sleep on the floor then."

"Remember, I got a knife."

While we polished off the remainder of the bottle he told me why he'd been sent away: two years for robbery with assault. He made no pretense of his innocence or that he was badly treated by the 'system.' In fact, he thought he got off lightly. There was also no regret and it was obvious he'd be back to his old life as soon as he made contact with his underworld mates.

While it was fun ogling the fucker, I couldn't get him to talk about what happened after lights went out in prison or what happened to cute young twinks in the shower. When he clammed up about such activities I yawned, telling him I had to get to bed.

"You really queer, mate?" he asked.

"Totally."

"You sure you're not fucking Kylie and pretending you're queer to save your skin?"

The idea was so ludicrous, I laughed. "My cock has never seen the inside of a cunt. Truth be known, I'm the kind of queer who likes to be on the receiving end and Kylie sure doesn't have the necessary equipment."

He picked up on that in quite the wrong way. "How do you know? When did you see her?" He sure wasn't the brightest match in the box.

"For fuck's sake lighten up, man. I didn't see her. She's a girl, right? Girls don't have cocks, right? Well, I love getting dicked up the ass."

"Don't it hurt?"

"Why, you thinking of trying it?"

I should have kept my smart ass comment to myself. He was up off his chair waving the knife in my general direction, too drunk to know what he was doing, which made him infinitely more dangerous and more appealing.

"I'm no fuckin' queer, mate."

"I know you're not. That was a joke."

"So you know I'm not queer? How can you tell?"

Oh, brother. I decided to lay it on thick.

"Just one look at you. You're one bad fucker. A man's man. The sort of guy that chicks fight over. The sort of man us poor queers worship but know we can't have. All we can do is look and dream about having a man like you pumping his dick into our throat, skull fucking us into submission, or banging our nelly assholes."

He smiled. "Yeah." Then adjusted his crotch.

He was quiet for a moment. I could almost hear the cogs of his brain, whirring. Planning.

"How about you let me watch you pushing that rubber thing up your ass. It'll remind me of Kylie. She liked to put on a show to get me off."

"I have to be in the mood for the large one and totally drug fucked. But I can accommodate the next size down."

"It's been two years, mate. Just me and my right hand and my imagination."

"You really wanna watch some filthy queer degrade himself in front of you by putting on a show, sticking I dunno what up his boy cunt so you can jerk your hard cock thinking of your girlfriend?"

I started slurring my speech so it sounded like I was as pissed as he was. Sounded less threatening to his fragile masculinity. I didn't doubt for a moment the guy was straight but I knew about situational homosexuality and he must have played the game in prison at least once or twice and if I could keep him on heat he might at least let me watch him jerk his meat because that morsel between his legs seemed to be stiffening by the second.

"You got anything better I can watch?" he demanded. "Porn, that sorta shit?"

I didn't have a TV or a player so he was out of luck there.

"I'd feel so fuckin' dirty knowing that a big hunk like you was watching me degrade myself. What choice do I have? You got a knife." I spoke softly, raising my voice several notches so I sounded more feminine. I minced over to the bedside table to switch on the lamp. "Honey, why don't you turn off the overhead so it's not so bright? That way I can put on a real good show for you. Here, make yourself comfortable." I plumped up a ratty cushion that had seen better days and pushed it to the back of the faded armchair that I had saved from a heap of furniture piled high on the footpath when one of the long-term residents had been locked out for non-payment of rent. I moved it to the end of the bed so he would have a perfect view.

As I rummaged through my toy drawer for props and the bottle of lube, my hand brushed against an item I had long forgotten. I'd found it under the bed when I first moved in, obviously it had been the property of the absconded Kylie.

"You almost ready?" he snapped. Obviously the sexual tension was getting to him.

"Nearly there, honey."

He smiled. "I like it when you call me 'honey.' Reminds me of Kylie."

"Why don't you strip out of those clothes, honey. Get yourself real comfortable."

That idea made him extra uncomfortable. He fidgeted. "That shit you snort. Better give me some of that. Might help."

I took two small bottles from the fridge, giving him the unopened one. It should blow the top right off his head. The other would do me because I was so buzzed that I hardly needed artificial stimulants.

As I stripped off my T-shirt I heard the hiss of his poppers being opened, followed by a right old snort or two. If that didn't do the trick nothing would.

I heard him mutter, "Holy shit!" as he struggled to remove his old clothes, falling into the chair half undressed. I bent over to remove the boxers I'd been sleeping in ensuring that he got a good glimpse of my smooth hairless buns. While my head was lowered I opened the tube of lipstick that I'd found and applied it to my mouth. My hair was naturally longish, students can't afford haircuts, and I hoped I looked sufficiently girly to pass in his frenzied state.

For a little extra courage I took a hit or two from my bottle and when I heard my heart pumping in my ears I stood up and turned to him.

His eyes opened to the size of saucers. "Shit, mate, you're fuckin gorgeous."

"Here, let me help you out of those uncomfortable old clothes of yours," I simpered as I kneeled in front of him, undoing the buttons on his shirt, taking the opportunity to flick each nipple, making him shudder. His body was wiry with scarcely any body fat. His muscles were pumped; obviously he spent a lot of time with weights while he was in prison. His arms carried the scars of inmate tattoos signifying gang allegiances and a crude sexual outline of a woman with big tits. The name Kylie was inked beneath it.

I held the poppers to his nose. "Here, honey. This will make you feel real good. Take a big sniff for Kylie."

Two snorts in each nostril and a beat or two before I leaned in to kiss the tat of Kylie. He groaned as I left the imprint of my lips. Then I turned my attention to his jeans. He'd managed to pull them part-way down.

"Here, shift your ass, honey, so I can get you out of these pants."

He lifted up, allowing me to drag down his jeans and his stained briefs. His cock popped free, fully hard, oozing its impatience, a nice thick morsel just ripe for my throat. He was still high so I quickly leaned in licked his cock slit, tasting his salty slime on my tongue.

He must have liked it because he kicked his trousers off fully to give himself more maneuverability before pushing two fingers inside my mouth stretching my lips apart. I sucked each digit, tasting the grime of his past, eager to get back to his cock.

"Let me take care of you, honey," I said, pushing him gently back against the chair. I cradled his balls in my hand as I placed my red lips over his nipple and sucked, nipping it slightly with my teeth. I repeated the exercise on the other nipple, and then traced my tongue down his chest toward his navel. It did the trick. He grabbed my head, moving it to his crotch. I opened wide and he plunged his prick straight down my gullet, choking me which seemed to please him. "Suck it, bitch. Give my cock a good workout. First decent blow job I had in years."

His cock was a work of art and I could have sucked it all night. If that's all I got I'd take it and be well pleased. But what I wanted more than anything was to feel his rod pounding my butthole.

Keeping his hands on the back of my head, he pushed me down to his balls stretching my throat around his cock, the lipstick smearing each time I slid up and down his slime pole. I knew he wouldn't last long if he hadn't been getting a lot of action in prison but I hoped he'd have enough in his balls for a back-up session. I was counting on it.

"Oh, baby, your mouth is so fuckin' sweet," he cooed.

I lifted my face off his knob which was leaking profusely from his piss slit. "Honey, you give me a mouthful of your hot man spunk and after I swallow it right down, you can plug my tight cunt hole with this big pole of yours."

"You fuckin' swallow? Oh shit. I wanna see that."

I spit bathed his cock until my drool was running down all over his balls but I didn't dare play with his butt even though I was desperate to ram my tongue into his hairy funk hole.

Turning my attention back to his cock, I ran my tongue over the sensitive knob before plunging my face down into his pubes.

"Holy shit, you got a velvet throat. Don't think I can take much more of it."

I wanted to prolong his enjoyment so I turned my attention back to his balls, slobbering spit all over them, and he moved down in the chair so I had better access. That gave me better access to his ass crack.

"Honey, why don't you take another snort or two because I'm gonna do something real special for ya. You'll love it so just relax."

He unscrewed the cap and took six large snorts offering me the bottle. I topped up my already wild libido and waited for the buzz to kick in. He moaned. I shifted his ass for better leverage. When I judged he was at the height of his buzz I parted his cheeks, sucked his wet hole and shoved my tongue in as far as I could go. He bucked, pushing himself back on my mouth so I could suck his asshole, smearing my face in his crack to get all his scent on my lips. I sucked and chewed his cunt until he was wriggling frantically trying to get away from my grip.

"That's so fuckin' intense," he groaned, jerking his cock. I knew if I wanted to taste his spunk I'd have to relinquish my grip on his ass. Coming up for air I put my mouth over his cock feeling the blood pumping that meant he was close to coming. I deep throated him once more for good luck then moved my lips back up to the top half of his prick, concentrating my tongue and suction action there.

It was a matter of moments before I felt the pulse catapulting up his cock shaft to splatter in my mouth. I sucked hungrily at the knob drawing out every spurt, storing it in my mouth to show him. When they subsided, I dragged my lips over the underside of his glans then across the crown until I'd suctioned up every bit of his juice.

I looked up at the ex-con, opening my mouth, sticky mucous stringing between my lips as the spunk puddled at the back of my throat, my tongue dripping spooge.

"Swallow it bitch. Show me how much you fuckin' love it."

I tasted the salty slime on my tongue then gulped it down like a giant mucous oyster slithering into my stomach.

"That's a good bitch," he smiled, thumbing my mouth open to make sure it was all down my gullet. I noticed his cock was still semi-hard so I hoped I still had a chance at getting him in my ass. There wouldn't be much foreplay but that was okay, all I wanted was slam/bam/no thanks necessary mam.

I grabbed the lube bottle, squished lube onto my fingers, and then lay back on the bed, lifting my legs so I could finger my hole, showing him how eager I was.

"You like my cunt, baby? Look how I like to feel my fingers inside. I wish it was a big man's cock."

He didn't bite, just sat there absent-mindedly playing with himself. I lubed my hole good, pulling the lips apart to get at the muscle inside. I ran my greasy fingers over one of my favorite dildos then, taking a quick hit of poppers, I placed the rubber cock against my ass entrance – and pushed. I gritted my teeth against the pain but felt my sphincter spread wide open to take the rubber intruder. I rested for a moment to get used to the pain. I was flying. Sure a rubber substitute is better than nothing when the real thing's not available but there was a perfectly good cock just feet away and I wanted it in my ass.

"Stroke that big hot cock, baby. Get it hard. Get it real hard. Imagine it's in my pussy, in my ass cunt. You feel so good inside me, honey. Going deep, fucking me rough like a real man does. Feel me gripping your shaft as you ram it in, filling me with your fuck seed."

I saw his eyes glaze over and his hand speed up.

"You like my pussy, honey? Yeah, hot pussy for your cock. Come on and fuck me, honey. Fuck me hard. You want my cunt, honey. Fill it with your huge fuckin' cock. I bet it won't even fit in my little hole but you'll force it in. Slam my hole. Come on fucker, shove it my cunt."

He stood up and kneeled on the bed behind me, yanking out the dildo, grabbing my waist, hoisting me over so my face was in the pillow. Without warning, his prick invaded my guts, plugging my hole totally. He didn't stop pushing until his stomach hit my ass. I was pinned to the bed unable to move except to push back against him.

"Holy fuck, you're tight. Hottest ass cunt I ever had."

I flexed my sphincter as he battered my hole, keeping up a barrage of cheap whore porn talk which he matched expletive for expletive. I couldn't have wished for a rougher lover. There was no finesse to his fucking, no consideration for me, his entire concentration was in his cock, and getting off regardless of whom or what was his partner. He was a sex animal and I loved it. I wanted it rough and that's how he was doing me. Downside: he wouldn't last long. Neither did I.

I felt his smaller load of hot spunk shoot inside my ass as I blew a stream of my own all over the blanket on my bed. He pulled out, sticky cum leaking down the back of my leg, and slapped my ass.

"Thanks, I needed that."

Without so much as a kiss or post-prandial cigarette, he got under the blankets and was asleep before I'd even tidied up. I took the time to empty my student cards and my sole credit card from my wallet leaving enough of my hard-earned cash that he wouldn't bother looking for any more before placing the wallet carefully on the table. It pays to be careful.

I wiped my ass but kept it lubricated before getting into bed but keeping far enough away from him as any sudden movement in my sleep and I'd be on the floor. My precautions were well justified because in the early hours of the morning I was awakened by the blunt head of his very hard cock pushing for entrance to my ass. I shifted enough to give him easy admission and he pounded into me as he held my throat. He didn't last long, shooting his load then rolling off me going back to sleep.

In the morning when I woke up, he was gone. So was my wallet.

I never bothered to repair the window, hoping, I suppose, for a return visit. But in the three years I lived there, it never happened again.

THE SKINHEAD UPSTAIRS

"Hold that lift!" The voice boomed through the deserted foyer. Automatically, I stuck my hand out to cut the beam so the door would remain open, but as soon as I saw who belonged to the voice, I regretted my politeness. Ever since the asshole had moved into the penthouse apartment above ours, we'd had nothing but aggravation.

He beamed as he shoved his way into the elevator, knocking me to the back wall with his body. Fucker!

"Thanks, faggot!" he spat as he poked the button for his own floor before I had a chance to press ours.

My boyfriend, Carlos, gripped my arm as a warning not to start a fight.

"Oh, ain't that sweet, the faggot's little fuck boy doesn't want any trouble."

He chucked Carlos under the chin like he was some kind of animal. "What's the matter, fuck boy? Scared of a real man?"

He flexed his arm, his bicep expanding like a small mountain, almost ripping his muscle T-shirt.

"Have a feel. That's real solid muscle. It'll make your little boy cunt juice up. Go on, put your hand on it."

I could sense Carlos wanted to take the dare; he'd always had a thing for muscles, something I'm rather scarce of, but his fear of the skinhead from upstairs and of my reaction made him hesitate.

"Don't be frightened of what Mr. Flabby here thinks. This is your once-in-a-lifetime opportunity to get up close to a fuckin' honest-to-god piece of real man flesh."

When Carlos still looked indecisive, Bull grabbed his hand and placed it on his bicep, flexing again. Carlos squeezed it timidly.

"Put some force into it, sweetheart. I'm not fragile like your boyfriend there."

Carlos squeezed again and I could see Bull's mouth form into a sneer.

"If you like that, babe, then you're gonna love these."

He lifted his T-shirt over his head, lodging it behind his neck so that his chest and abdomen were shown off to great effect. I had to bite my tongue to stop myself from gasping.

"That's it, baby. Have a good feel, store up those sensations so next time your piss weak shit of a lover is fucking his teeny weenie in that nasty little ass of yours…" To emphasize his point, Bull squeezed Carlos's butt making my boyfriend squeal. "Good little faggot fuck pig. I'll let you dream it's this body pressing against you."

Bull ran Carlos's hand across his hairy pecs, and then down over his chiseled abs. Carlos was having problems controlling his breathing. The bully took his hand off Carlos's just as it reached the waist band of his slung-too-low gym shorts so my boyfriend was free to move it any which way he desired. There was a tense stand-off. The atmosphere in the elevator was ripe with testosterone. Sure, I could have wrenched Carlos's hand away from the skinhead's body but I was rather intrigued what he would do next.

Bull was so supremely confident. "Go on, I know you want to. You won't get another chance like this, fag boy. Your last chance to feel a real man's cock." He began to move slowly to remove my boyfriend's hand from his body. At the last possible moment, Carlos slid his hand beneath the shorts and down to the creep's cock letting out a gasp of surprise as he obviously found more than he'd expected.

"Feel something you like?"

He didn't need a reply, it was all-too-obvious that Carlos had found something very much to his liking.

"Bet you've never had one as juicy as that before," Bull teased, attempting to humiliate me further. "Why not have a little taste. That's it, rub your fingers around the head, get all that drooling pre-cum on your fingers."

There seemed to be a lot of movement in Bull's shorts before Carlos withdrew his hand, his fingers glistening.

He stared at them for the longest time, the humiliating silence broken by the snapped command, "Go on, you know what to do with it."

Carlos pushed his fingers into his mouth and sucked, his eyes closed as if in hog heaven.

"You've got a cute ass, fag boy, and my cock ain't always fussy. Especially if there's no pussy around. Any time you want some action from a real man who knows how to treat a filthy fag slut, come on up, the door's always open if I'm home." He turned to me, then grabbed my crotch in his powerful hands, squeezing until my balls felt fit to burst. "Yeah, I thought so. Fuckin' turns you on. Who knows, I might even let you watch."

He laughed like the devil as we reached his floor and he got out. In the brief seconds before the door closed, he turned to look at Carlos, sneering as he said, "Think about it, boy." It wasn't a suggestion, it was a command.

The lift went back down to our floor below. When we reached our apartment, I was shaking so badly Carlos had to help with the key. He seemed much less fazed by the confrontation with our nemesis than I was.

"You wouldn't, would you?" I asked Carlos. I felt pretty confident because the guy was as ugly as a hatful of assholes and I was pretty sure of my own good looks. I just needed to hear Carlos's assurances, particularly as I felt vulnerable in the cock size department and in my ability to protect my boyfriend in a face-to-face fight with Bull.

Carlos snorted, "Of course not. He's an animal."

We'd had problems with him since the day he arrived. Then he had looked an unlikely tenant of the luxurious penthouse on the eighteenth floor that overlooked the park and had a spectacular view of the mountains in the west. It had taken every penny we possessed to snag the apartment directly below, the one above with a price tag of at least two million was way more than we could afford.

That first night, Bull threw a housewarming party and as his sundeck was directly above our bedroom ceiling there was no chance we'd get any sleep until it stopped. The whir of his Jacuzzi, the tramp of shoes across the wooden floor planks, the shrieks of boozy laughter, and the whoomph of the bass beat almost drove us mad.

Earlier that day, we'd watched the removalist's van deliver high end furnishings leading to expectations that a successful IT nabob or a company CEO had taken up residence although the removal men themselves were a rag-tag bunch, especially the shaven-headed foreman whose frequent use of the foulest expletives turned the air blue. When one of our women neighbors stuck her head over the balcony to remonstrate with him, explaining she didn't want her children to hear that sort of language, he called her a 'cunt' and told her to mind her 'own fuckin' business.'

She informed him she was calling the company to complain.

"You do that," he called up to her.

He either didn't care about his job or else was indispensable to the company. We found out later which it was when we took up a hamper of goodies as a welcome to the neighborhood when we heard the new owner moving about on the sun deck later in the day.

As his is the only residence on the eighteenth floor, we were unsurprised that his door was wide open, revealing the normal clutter of someone who has just moved residences. The apartment itself was eerily quiet so we knocked loudly.

"What the fuck?"

The voice and tone were all-too-familiar. Carlos clutched my arm, trying to pull me back to the lift, but before he could make his escape the skinhead removalist came striding toward us, his lace-up bovver boots, clacking across the floor's marble tiles.

"Oh," he muttered when he saw we came bearing gifts. "Are you the official welcoming committee?"

"No, we're just being neighborly."

"You're the two fags who live beneath me." He laughed. "Just my little joke. Fags are always beneath somebody." He looked at our grim faces. "Not funny? Who gives a shit?"

"We were hoping to greet the new owner," I said. "We'll come back some other time when he's home. Sorry to disturb you."

"You've met him," he sneered. "I'm not good enough for your pissy little neighborhood, is that it?"

"No, it's just…" I stopped. He was right, I'd made assumptions. Just like I'd assumed he was a skinhead because his scalp was clean shaven, he wore his jeans tucked into his ass-kicker boots, and he had military-style tattoos on his upper arms. One or two of them looked suspiciously like Nazi iconography. But it was his head, tattooed with bizarre symbols that made him appear really evil. In fact, if you stared long enough, they took on the appearance of a satanic face. As well, he had symbols down one cheek. He definitely looked like someone we didn't want in our building.

"To save you wondering, I sold my soul to the devil when I was ten. This was all he asked when I was sixteen. He'll do anything for me. How else could I afford to live here?"

"Come on, let's go," Carlos looked petrified.

"So the nasty little fuck toy can actually speak? For a moment I thought he was just a realistic-looking blow-up doll. Well, I guess he is. I bet the whole faggy area has blown up his ass one time or another."

"Just a minute," I said, drawing myself up to my full height which still only reached his chest. I was prepared to fight for my man, but I knew I'd be the very sore loser. So did Carlos.

"Come on, Liam, It's not worth it."

"You think not, fag boy." He grabbed a handful of his own crotch. "You don't know how wrong you are."

Of course, since the more recent incident in the lift, Carlos did know how wrong he was.

Those first few weeks after he moved in, the noise drove us both spare as did the constant taunting of Bull's mates who seemed to come and go with monotonous regularity. We tried complaining to building management, among the many to do so, but they maintained it wasn't their job. The woman I spoke to sounded scared to even discuss the topic. The police, when we'd finally had enough and called them, were openly bored. "Look, mate, we get so many complaints like yours from all over, I can sprout the usual bullshit that I'll send someone around but chances are the noise will have stopped by the time one of our cars gets there."

I was not about to be fobbed off so lightly, insisting it was the duty of the police to protect innocents like ourselves from bullying. I threatened to take out an apprehended violence order which would make the cops' job even harder.

"Okay, give me the address." When I told him, he said, "Oh, we've had lots of complaints from there." He sighed down the phone which seemed to imply that he'd have to do something about it.

By the time I hung up I'd received assurances that, barring a terrorist attack on the city, the cops would be there within two hours. I knew from experience the party noise would not have died down by then and the constant ebb and flow of unsavory characters visiting the penthouse would not have slowed.

Carlos and I were watching from the balcony when the police car pulled up in the street below and two young cops swaggered to the front of the building. I heard the squawk of the buzzer as they pressed for admission to the apartment upstairs, the sound of loud music ricocheting across the street from the intercom.

"It'll be over soon and we can get some sleep," Carlos smiled, patting me affectionately on the back because he knew how wound up I was by the disturbance. Fifteen minutes later there was no change to the relentless sound of partying, in fact I thought it had increased in volume so that I almost missed the knocking at our apartment door. I didn't for a minute believe that Bull and his mates had waylaid the cops and chopped them into tiny pieces and that he was now outside our front door about to wreak his revenge for our complaints, but the thought did flitter across my mind.

I opened the door on the two police who had the decency to look embarrassed.

"We asked him to tone it down, mate," one of the cops said. "He just told us to fuck off."

"That's it?" I asked, scarcely containing my disgust.

"Look, we've had so many complaints about the noise, and his personal behavior. Some people in the building have tried to take out an AVO against him."

I waited for him to go on but he just stared at me as if he'd said all there was to say. When I just looked at him blankly, it must have registered that I expected more. He looked surprised. "Don't you know who the guy is?" My open-mouthed stare must have told him that I didn't. Before he and his fellow cop turned on their heels and went back down the corridor leaving me bewildered, he mentioned a name which meant nothing to me, then added, "You're on your own, mate."

Carlos and I logged on to Google his name, discovering there were enough references to our irritating neighbor to fill an encyclopedia.

Sal 'The Bull' Santi.

I yanked my fingers off the keyboard as soon as the first hit came up on the screen, followed by thousands more. Shit! My heart sank, along with the value of our apartment, as I read up on his history. At least now we discovered how he could afford to buy the penthouse apartment, plus why the police had been too timid to do anything about him.

Sal Santi was known as a major crime figure but had managed, through the connivance of smart lawyers as well as corrupt cops and court officials, to keep out of prison. He'd been harassed by the law and even been arrested on drugs charges after huge quantities of heroin and cocaine had been discovered in one of his warehouses. The gleeful cops had been rather too rash in arresting him, and a little too brutal in their interrogation. They were also much too lax in allowing the closed circuit surveillance in the cop station to capture their rather unusual interview technique which strayed so far outside what was acceptable to their departmental superiors that a number of officers were demoted or dismissed.

Naturally enough, Sal screamed harassment, police brutality and wrongful arrest. Once a young cop rolled over for the Police Integrity Commission in exchange for clemency and revealed the drugs had been planted on Sal's premises by the cops themselves, the shit really hit the fan. The ultimate pay-out, once Bull's lawyer's had finished shredding reputations in an effort to make his client sound like a second cousin to Mother Teresa, was rumored to be in the range of seven figures. The judge in the case was particularly scathing at about the rogue activity against such an upstanding citizen who was a generous supporter of various charities and youth sporting organizations.

No wonder no one was prepared to risk a charge of harassment, the police department keeping him at arm's length from that time on. It looked as if that was our only course of action as well. We'd just have to put up with it.

Climbing the stairs to avoid Bull was not an option as we were too high up, so occasionally Carlos or I would run into him in the elevator, like the occasion on which he invited Carlos to 'feel him up.' We also had the misfortune to run into his mates, a rowdy bunch of faggot baiters who were even more aggressive and loathsome than Bull, probably because they spurred one another on to grosser insults. Carlos, in particular, was at their mercy because he used the underground car park more than I did, as well as popping down to our storage cage for items he suddenly needed for various functions around the apartment.

I found out just how gross their actions were one evening when Carlos came home obviously distressed and disheveled, his face plastered with slime.

"They cursed me," he groaned. "Called me all sorts of filthy names. One of them even took his cock out and waved it in my face telling me to 'come and get it.' They laughed at me, forcing me down onto my knees. He hit me over the face with his cock, sneering at me for being a weak faggot."

Carlos's voice became heavy and breathless as he told me of his humiliation at the hands of Bull's buddies. I knew he was on the verge of tears.

"They called me a 'fuck toy' and told me I was theirs to use if they ever ran into me again. All faggots are good for is a hole to dump cum and piss in. Then they forced me…"

He was so distraught he couldn't go on. He looked at me with horror in his eyes.

"What must you think of me, Liam?"

"What's the slime on your face, Carlos?"

"Ah…they spat on me. They all stood around me and…spat on me. Then the leader made me open my mouth and he…spat on my tongue, telling me to hold it there then he forced his…he pissed in my mouth and made me swallow it. Then they all…um…spat on me."

Carlos covered his face and ran to the bathroom in shame.

My blood boiled that they could do such a thing to my darling boyfriend. I gave him his privacy, waiting until he emerged from the bathroom, his face now clean of his submission, his spirits much less the worse for wear.

"What are we going to do, Carlos?" I asked.

"Nothing at all," he said calmly.

"There must be security footage of the attack, after all the car park has a number of cameras. We could take it to the police. I'm sure they'd love to have evidence against Bull's lieutenants."

Carlos appeared panic-stricken for a moment, as if he hadn't thought about his brutal subjugation being captured as evidence. "We don't want to antagonize them further," he said. "That would only bring Bull down on our heads. He's not a man to be messed with."

"I'll make sure I come with you if you ever need to go down to the car park, okay?"

He looked aghast at the prospect. "What sort of signal does that send?" he said. "That will just confirm that I'm scared and what a chicken shit little faggot I am."

"Don't say that about yourself," I snapped.

"There's no point in stirring the pot. There are more of them than there are of us. They didn't actually hurt me," he said, attempting to placate me. "I'm all right, honestly."

But he wasn't all right. Any time I attempted to instigate lovemaking after that, Carlos would plead that the scars of his humiliation made it impossible to give me the full attention that I deserved. I knew he was raw psychologically, even suggesting that he seek counseling, particularly after he became obsessive about clearing out our storage cage so he would not have to go into the garage except to get his car. He began to spend up to an hour at time, sorting through the collected detritus of our life together, neatly boxed and labeled in storage.

I was pleased because it was a task we'd both put off in the years we'd been in residence and it was helping Carlos confront his fears. He'd also begun visiting the gym and even though he was still untouchable to me because of his psychological bruising, his body took on a definition it never had before. I could scarcely keep my hands off him, wanting more than anything to sink my cock in his increasingly bubbly butt. When it all became too much for me, he would take me in his warm mouth, deep throating me with a skill I had not known him to possess before.

When I complained I needed more, he would just suck deeper and later whisper, "Soon, Liam. Very soon."

Soon seemed to be a subjective term as he spent longer periods in the storage area. He also spent what I considered an inordinate amount of time in the car park washing and polishing his vehicle which was nothing out of the ordinary – he'd bought it second hand.

Sometimes he'd come back to the apartment and I knew he'd had problems with Bull or his mates as he'd have strings of slime across his face where they'd obviously spat on him and he hadn't cleaned it off carefully enough. I realized he was attempting to spare me his humiliating experiences in a futile attempt to keep the peace, but my heart broke when I saw my man treated with such contempt. One day I would fight back, then watch out.

For all his trouble, Carlos blossomed, becoming more confident, more forgiving of our upstairs neighbor's transgressions, while I brooded, ready to explode at the most trivial provocation.

He shrugged it off when Bull used the Jacuzzi but the vibrations down our walls, sent me mental. "We've got to get used to it. No use getting all uptight about something you can't control. Don't fight it. If you don't let it worry you, then it's not a problem."

"How very Zen," I replied with as much sarcasm as I could muster.

He started wearing ear plugs to bed to block out the noise of any partying but I found doing the same was disorientating and mucked up the rest of my day. As Carlos developed an ability to cope with the increasing provocation I began falling apart.

It all culminated one Saturday night after I'd had the week from hell at work, brought on to a large extent by my obsessing over Bull and my lack of real sex from Carlos. This had become months of solo wanking in the shower and I was edgy the whole time. I was ready to snap, so when the shouts and yahoos from upstairs were joined by the sound of the hot tub throbbing down the wall next to my pillow, I screamed.

It penetrated the foam earplugs that Carlos swore by, waking him. He could see the anger and despair in my eyes which he attempted to soothe with a mug of hot chamomile tea. It did the trick for about five minutes. It calmed me enough that I didn't march right upstairs and attempt to rip Bull's head off. Still, we were no closer to a solution to our problem.

Sighing deeply, I said, "Why don't I just go upstairs and admit defeat. See if there's some compromise we can hammer out. See if we can make a deal whereby we can live in some sort of truce, if not harmony."

"I think that's a good idea," Carlos agreed. "But I don't think it's wise for you to go up there tonight. You're all wound up and just as likely to make the situation worse. Wait until your mind is clearer. Better yet, why don't I go upstairs and see if I can negotiate?"

"I don't like the idea of you going alone. We should both go," I said.

"Why don't you take one of your sleeping tablets, get a good night's sleep. It'll do you the world of good."

Carlos went to the bathroom, returning with two of my little pills and a glass of water. "Here you go," he said.

I didn't like the idea of having to rely on medication to get what should, by rights, have come naturally but for the excessive noise from upstairs. Carlos had picked the less severe tablets that gave me a few hours' sleep rather than the stronger ones which laid me out for around eight hours. The only downside to the pills he'd given me was the groggy and disoriented state they left me in when I awoke.

Carlos kissed me, squeezing my cock affectionately. The last thing I remember is him putting in his ear plugs and lying beside me.

It was 2am when I awoke, startled by screams from the street and the slamming of car doors which meant the party upstairs was winding down. Rolling over to seek solace in a cuddle with Carlos, I was surprised his side of the bed was empty. I wandered groggily through the apartment searching for him, expecting that he'd got up to use the toilet or to watch a program on early morning television because he'd run out of sleep. He was nowhere to be found.

Sly dog. He must have gone upstairs to complain, his results much better than mine would have been. He has a more amenable manner, compromising when he has to while I'm more like a bull at a gate. Although the noisy revelers had quieted the hot tub still vibrated down the walls but I expected that to cut off shortly. I brewed a pot of Carlos's favorite coffee so he could tell me all about his journey into the lair of the skinhead upstairs, but when he hadn't returned twenty minutes later and the vibrations down the wall were threatening my sanity, I decided enough was enough.

Screwing up my courage and swathing it in anger, all the time wondering what had become of Carlos, I stormed out to the lift, jabbing the button as if it were my enemy. When it took too long to get to my floor and frightened my resolve would wither and die, I slammed through the door to the fire stairs and taking two steps at a time made my way to the floor above. I admit I was trembling, hoping nothing had happened to Carlos, if he was even up there, and that I had the balls not to capitulate to Bull's threats.

As he'd once told us, the door to his apartment was wide open although there was no one around, the party obviously having disbanded.

Do I knock? It's difficult to make an aggressive entrance when you knock on an open door. Do I storm in? I may end up looking like a knob. God, I am so indecisive.

Plucking up my courage, after all I could come out of this with broken limbs and a black eye or two if Bull took exception to my complaints, I strode into the apartment determined to stand my ground. The apartment itself dazzled. I hadn't been up here since the ill-advised welcoming. Bull had exquisite taste and in my admiration I almost lost my impetus, until I heard the sound of laughter and the whining buzz that did my head in.

Gritting my teeth, I ignored the furnishings and art that normally would have occupied me for hours. Summoning up determination, I burst from the living area onto the sun deck, now illuminated by strings of subdued lighting strung along beams over the party area. Bull was lounging in the hot tub, beer in hand, guffawing at something his companion must have said. I was distressed to find that companion was none other than my own beloved, Carlos, who had the decency to look shocked to have me catch him fraternizing with the enemy. How could he be so chummy with the man who constantly belittled us as faggots and whose mates had abused him physically?

Before I could let fly with my accusations, Bull motioned me over. "Come on in and join us."

I was in no mood for his sneering put-downs but Carlos's eyes pleaded with me to be nice. I don't like being on unsure ground and there was nothing more treacherous than the ground upon which I now stood. I decided discretion was better than temper, walking to the edge of the tub wondering what the hell people wore in a situation like this.

"Hop in," Bull invited.

It did look inviting and I noticed the calm look on Carlos's face even as his cheeks were flamed red, which I put down to the glass of white wine he was imbibing. "I didn't bring—" I objected.

"None necessary," Bull said, standing to confirm it, his cock bloody impressive at half-mast. No wonder Carlos had been enthralled. Against my average-sized cock, Bull's was a Nobel prizewinner. He shifted closer to Carlos to give me room. Much too close to my boyfriend for my liking.

"Come on, Liam. It'll relax you after your bad week at the office," Carlos cajoled.

What did I have to lose? Just a cock comparison, muscle comparison, but each of us already knew that. I shrugged and removed my clothes, folding them over the metal chairs of the sun deck furniture and then slid into the warm bubbling water, seating myself on the small wooden ridge than ran the circumference of the tub.

"Isn't that better?" Carlos said cheerfully.

I had to admit, if only to myself, it was. The tension slowly seeped out of me, my shoulders relaxed, the terrible crick in my neck slowly unknotted as the water in the tub seduced me, making me even more sluggish in my reactions.

"Get your boyfriend a white wine, Carlos," Bull commanded, and soon enough I was sipping a very superior chardonnay. I asked for the bottle and was impressed that it was the Lane RG Vineyard 2009. I topped up my glass before handing the bottle back. Under normal circumstances, Carlos and I could never afford wine of this standard. Perhaps I had misjudged Bull. Taking another sip, I slipped further into the warm comforting embrace of the tub.

"Shit hot booze, eh, Liam?" Bull smiled.

It was not a convincing smile, it looked more like the toothy grin of some vicious creature that was about to devour you. That should have warned me but what with the warm seductive embrace of the water and the almost lethal combination of sleeping tablets and booze, I was well on the way to oblivion.

We exchanged pleasantries about nothing in particular although I'm afraid I gushed over his good taste.

"I presume you got decorators in?"

It was a nasty putdown but I simply couldn't imagine the huge tattooed hulk having the capacity for such refinement. He didn't flinch, so he was either more stupid than I gave him credit for or else he was saving it up for later.

"No, I chose all that shit myself, all the furniture, all the art. Plus this wine. Of course, it helps to have money when you have expensive tastes like I do. Plus a fine eye for beauty. Like young Carlos here." So saying, Bull wrapped his big beefy arms around my boyfriend, pulling him closer.

I expected some sort of remonstration from Carlos but there was nothing except a sly smirk at the compliment.

I was about to object that he was pawing my boyfriend but as Carlos himself was not objecting it seemed petty. Besides, Bull got in first. "He tells me you've been neglecting him of late. What's the matter with you, mate, leaving your little faggot boy to get his pleasure elsewhere?"

I should have known the truce wouldn't last. I stood up to grab Carlos and leave but in my wobbly state it was easy for Bull to push me back down with his foot. "Sit down and shut the fuck up."

I waited for Carlos to come to my defense but he merely stared at me as if interested to see my reaction. My head was fuzzy, my body felt like lead, I was having difficulty focusing. What did he mean by 'get his pleasure elsewhere'?

I didn't have time to ponder it, as Bull turned his vindictive personality on me full force.

"Stand up, Carlos," Bull commanded. "Show Liam what a hot little body you have. It's been so long he's probably forgotten what it's like."

How did Bull know how long it's been? And it was hardly my neglect, it was Carlos's reluctance. Carlos had obviously been discussing our private life. That was unforgiveable.

I was about to protest but Bull said, "Carlos, bend over, show Liam what he's been neglecting."

As my boyfriend stood to do as Bull demanded, I snapped, "Carlos!"

They both ignored me.

"Pull your cheeks apart, boy," Bull said.

Carlos reached back and squeezed his butt open so I could see his beautiful anal bud.

"Kiss it, Liam."

It was a breathtaking sight, the hot moist hole I'd been denied for so long. Without thinking, I kneeled and ran my tongue up that amazing crevasse then licked down again until I reached the hole, poking my tongue into the sphincter to lube it so I could slip inside. I chewed the puckered lips, wetting them with my saliva until Carlos was groaning, forcing his butt harder against my mouth. I sucked his asshole until he was loose and sloppy, until my tongue forced its way into his bowels and I tasted…what was that? No, it couldn't be. We'd both sworn at the beginning of our relationship that if we ever slipped up in our troth of monogamy, we'd play safe. I sucked his ass again. Although there was a pungent taste I knew it couldn't be what my paranoia was suggesting.

"I see you like that, Liam."

There was no use denying it as my rigid cock gave me away.

"Squeeze some more out for your boyfriend, Carlos. Looks like he's hungry." Bull was obviously enjoying himself.

I'd felt Carlos attempting to clamp his sphincter closed even as I was invading him with my tongue. He had something to hide and I'd tasted it. Now that he'd been given the all-clear, he relaxed and I felt man slime ooze into my mouth. I spluttered as I swallowed, frightened I would throw up.

I couldn't show any sign of weakness to the skinhead.

"Come and sit on my lap, fag boy," Bull commanded.

Carlos turned to look at me. I must have been a pitiful sight kneeling in the hot tub, my mouth shiny with the slime from his ass. If he was waiting for a sign, my obvious submissive posture probably gave him his answer. He shrugged and moved over to Bull who grabbed his waist to guide him down.

"Hey, faggot," Bull called to me. "Get your flabby ass over here."

I crawled across to where Bull was seated.

"Hold my cock steady and guide it into your boyfriend's fuck hole," he ordered.

I baulked, about to refuse, but his hand shot out grabbing my throat in a powerful grip. "Unless you want to end up at the bottom of the harbor, faggot, you'll do as I say. Understand?"

I couldn't speak, so I nodded my head.

"Good faggot." He patted me on the head to show his complete domination of me.

I reached over and placed my hand around Bull's substantial prick as Carlos lowered his body toward it. Feeling for his butt hole, I guided the cock to it and felt it sink all the way in to the balls. My boyfriend grimaced for a moment, I heard his intake of breath, then the pain must have subsided.

Bull addressed me as Carlos bobbed up and down impaling himself on skinhead prick. "Pity you turned up, faggot. You've spoiled a good thing. You probably thought that was my spunk you tasted in your slut boyfriend's ass. Not this time although he's been draining my balls on a regular basis like a good cocksucking fag slut should. You know all those nights you grizzled about the hot tub? That was my signal to your fag boy to get his ass upstairs. Me and my buddies have been tagging him at both ends for weeks."

What could I say? My mouth opened and closed without uttering a word. I was too numb to comprehend everything just yet. "It was me who insisted Carlos stop taking you in his ass. I didn't want to stick my cock where some putrid weak fag like you had dumped his load. We worked him over in the car park a couple of times. I made sure he wore some of my cock snot proudly on his face when he went home to you, pussy."

Carlos's eyes were rolling back in his head which meant Bull's cock was hitting all the right spots.

"You like watching your sweet little slut take a real man's cock in his tight butt? Yeah, I knew you would. If you're real good, I'll let you watch me and my mates fuck the shit out of your little boyfriend here. When we've finished with him, you can have him back. Of course, he'll be all fucked out and his hole will be gaping because we have a few ideas about what we'd like to see shoved up there." To emphasize his point he held his fist up. "Now wouldn't that be a sight? Little Carlos's ass muscles wrapped around my bicep. Fuck, eh?"

I felt so helpless watching Bull ram his cock in and out of the ass that had been exclusively mine until recently.

"You want my cock, boy?" Bull asked.

"Yes, sir. I love the feel of your hard cock in my tiny hole."

"Is my cock better than your boyfriend's?"

"Fuck, yeah," Carlos said, looking at me piteously. "Your cock is the best ever, sir. It's like I'm being fucked by the devil himself."

At that moment the lights seemed to fade and Bull stood up in the hot tub, Carlos carried aloft by his thick, hard cock. The man was pure evil. I saw the veins in his head pulse, the tattoo on his forehead took on a ghastly appearance, I could have sworn I saw a horned face when I stared at the pattern long enough. I put my wine down, my mind was playing tricks on me. There was the sound of guests coming from inside and soon three of Bull's homophobic mates spilled out onto the sundeck.

"Hey, you started without us," one of them said.

Another saw me. "Shit, what's he doing here?"

"Don't worry, guys, the faggot loves to see his cheating slut boyfriend with foreign cock in his ass. Don't you, fag?"

I nodded my head.

"Can't hear you," Bull chanted as he pushed Carlos over the edge of the tub. "Len, fill his mouth, mate." Then he turned back to me, "Still can't hear you."

"Yes," I mumbled.

"Oh, oh," one of the other mates muttered.

The hand was around my throat again before I even saw it coming. "You will refer to me as 'sir' or 'master' in future? Understand?"

"Yes…sir," I said, my humiliation complete.

"Good fag. How about you help my mates out while I finish off in the little fag's blow hole. Nick, Reg, use the fag boyfriend's mouth any way you want. Choke the fucker for all I care." Bull turned back to Carlos. "Sweet baby fag, your ass is on fire."

Nick shoved his cock down my throat without any preliminaries.

"You know," Bull crowed, "You would have enjoyed watching your little boy here take on the guys at the party. Insatiable little slut, lay on his back in the living room so we could use him as our pissoir all evening. Right, Carlos?" The subject of his story had no hope of answering because Len had skewered his throat so that tears and puke were streaming from the corners of his mouth and out his nose as his breath was choked off.

"His mouth was our trough. He drank us down until his stomach was so distended he looked like he was fuckin' pregnant. What a sight that was, eh guys?"

They all mumbled their agreement.

"Of course we didn't neglect his asshole, not like you have been. Hell, no. We know your little fag likes nothing better than to have cock shoved up his ass. Am I right, Liam?"

I did my best to say "Yes, sir," which enabled Nick to push his cock so far down my throat I thought I'd never survive.

"What do you think of your boyfriend now, baby fag?" Bull asked, nodding at Len to remove his cock from Carlos's mouth.

Ted pulled his cock out of my mouth, pulling my hair so that I looked into my boyfriend's eyes. I was horrified to see the contempt there.

"Show him how much you despise him, baby fag," Bull encouraged.

I heard the telltale sounds of Carlos hawking up his saliva in a ball. He sneered as he blew the wad out his mouth and straight onto my cheek.

The men applauded his aim.

"What do you think of your boyfriend now, slut?"

Carlos spat at me again. "Useless fuckin' faggot. You're like all faggots, just a hole for real men to stick their cocks in." Bull was milking Carlos's cock while he had his own buried to the hilt in my boyfriend's ass. "You thought you were so bloody superior when you fucked me with your puny prick, but I always dreamed of a real mancock like Bull's. He can make me beg just by slamming his prick in my guts. You never made me scream. I faked it most of the time. Weak fuckin' faggot."

Bull nodded at his offsiders who grabbed me, wrestling me onto my back on the wooden slats of the sun deck, hoisting my ass into the air.

"Show him, baby fag," Bull said.

Carlos seemed like he was mesmerized as he stepped from the tub, his cock now rampant. He eyed my butthole which he'd never shown any interest in fucking before. I struggled because it was not something I enjoyed, but there was no escape.

"Show him, fag boy," Bull encouraged.

Carlos was like a man on autopilot. He spat in my ass, pushing it in with his fingers, burning my sphincter with his intrusion. A little more saliva was all the lubrication he allowed before he thrust deep inside giving me no time at all to adjust to the searing pain.

The guys surrounded us, chanting "Fuck him! Fuck him! Fuck him!" as my boyfriend pounded my shit chute like a man possessed.

"How do you like it, slut?" Carlos spat at me. "Feel good having a cock buried in your fag cunt? We're gonna breed you, make you a fuck toy for all master's men. They'll love how tight you feel. They'll love choking you on their strong, hard cocks. You'll love it just like I love the feel of cock all over my body. The feel of warm spunk covering your face. You'll beg for it, baby."

I no longer recognized the man who was pounding into me as Carlos. Saddened as I was by the loss of my mate, I was getting excited by the dick wedged in my ass, his breath labored as he neared his peak. "I'm gonna spooge inside your ass, mate. Feel me blow my load, breeding your ass." He grunted to the applause of the men watching. I couldn't hold off any longer and squirted my juice all over my chest and stomach.

Carlos pulled out. "Wow, the fucker's tight. You'll enjoy him, master."

"Okay, boys, he's all yours," Bull said, his mates crowding around for a turn at my mouth or my ass. I was a leaking cum dump by the time they'd finished with me, spurred on by a vindictive Carlos. Then it was Bull's turn and I was grateful for his henchmen opening me up and lubricating me with their spunk before he stabbed his huge cock into my guts. I screamed but it did no good because Bull kept right on fucking me, his hideous satanic face poised over mine as I begged for mercy. He showed none, branding me as his possession with his scalding sperm.

It was morning by the time Carlos and I crawled back to bed in our apartment downstairs, sleeping in the slime cover as instructed by Bull. Of course, there was no way our relationship could survive but it limped on for a few weeks until I came home one day and Carlos's possessions were all missing. I thought he may have moved upstairs but I was soon disabused of that. No matter, I felt nothing for him anymore.

Eventually, my life assumed its mantle of normality again, except now I worked out at the gym as much as possible to keep my body toned. I'll never be as built as Bull but it's something I can aspire to. I got used to the noise from his parties and now even the vibration of his Jacuzzi starting up is music to my ears. It's my signal from the master to get my ass upstairs.

ABOUT THE AUTHOR

Barry Lowe writes about love and sex so he won't forget how to do it. When he's not scribbling his adventures for the Sydney gay weekly SX, or out doing field research, he's writing about love's wonderful variations for a series of smut eBooks, novels and anthologies for Lydian Press.

Go to www.barrylowe.info

OTHER WORKS BY BARRY LOWE

NOVELS & ANTHOLOGIES
Available in eBook and Print

BUSTING BILLY'S BUTT: A Gay Erotic Romance

Steve and Billy's monogamous relationship has gone stale until Billy, ever the exhibitionist, shows them a way to spice up their sex life.

THE MAJOR AND THE MINERS: A Gay Historical Romance

1930s Australia: Two men from opposite ends of the social spectrum. Is love enough to overcome the obstacles between them?

THE GRAVY TRAIN: A Murder Mystery with Recipes

Someone on the train has an appetite for murder!

A TOUCH OF THE SON: A Gay Novel

Their secret passion will lead them to hell. Will they be able to find their way back?

ROMANCING THE BONE: Gay Romance Erotica

OMG! NOT ANOTHER GAY EROTICA ANTHOLOGY?

ROUGH & READY: Gay Tough Guy Erotica

YOUR BOYFRIEND IS HOT: Gay Cuckold Erotica

BEAR SKIN: Hot Gay Bear Erotica

THE MORE THE MERRIER: Gay Gangbang Erotica

THE BOY IS A BOTTOM: Gay Anal Erotica

COCK-EYED OPTIMISTS: Gay Romance Erotica

BABY, I'M NOT A MONSTER: Gay Vampire and Other Paranormal Erotica

SHORT FICTION
Available as eBooks

TUNNEL VISION

HARD ON HIS HEELS

SPIN THE BOTTOM

THE NEW DAD'S CLUB

FOUR ON THE FLOOR

TAGGED BY THE TEAM

For all Barry's titles please visit his page at:
lydianpress.com

Lydian Press is dedicated to bringing you the
finest GLBTQ erotic literature on the web.

Visit us on the web at:
http://lydianpress.com